# GOTHIC TALES OF TERROR

# Gothic Tales of Terror

edited by
Krista Clark Grabowski

Gothic Tales of Terror
Book © Verto Publishing 2015

http://www.vertopublishing.com/
https://www.facebook.com/vertopublishing
Twitter: @vertopublishing

ISBN-13: 978-0692564271
ISBN-10: 0692564276

Edited and compiled by Krista Clark Grabowski

Assistant Editors L. E. Fitzpatrick and Elisha Murphy

Cover design © John D. Stanton

Illustrations for The Grinning Cat, and Speech to the Prometheus League © Joshua L. Hood

Illustrations for Hollenstein and The House that Jack Built © P. Emerson Williams

Photo following Table of Contents as well as photos for The Governess, the Revenant of Shelby House, and Who Will Die Tonight © John D. Stanton

This book is a work of fiction. Any references to historical events, real people, or real locales are used fictitiously. Any resemblance to actual events, or persons, living or dead, is coincidental.

# Table of Contents

# ACKNOWLEDGEMENTS

This particular project was great fun for me as the horror I enjoy most is subtle horror. Horror with an eerie and mysterious feeling that doesn't need gore in order to frighten is my favorite. And I have always loved anything Victorian. Gothic Tales of Terror incorporates both of these elements.

The creation of any published book is a journey from concept to finished product. There are many stops along the journey, many steps to be taken, and virtually none of them can be done alone if they are to be done well. Some of the people I'd like to thank for assistance in this particular project are:

James Ward Kirk who showed confidence in my writing and editing abilities a couple of years ago and gave me the confidence to pursue my passion. Thanks to him also for his help with a variety of items related to the production of this book.

Mike Jansen who is my Kindle expert. Thanks for your patience with me and for being willing to answer my many questions.

L. E. Fitzpatrick and Elisha Murphy, my assistant editors, who are always eager to help in whatever task I ask them to help and who have proven to be excellent editors as well as moral supporters.

John D. Stanton who is the expert I always know I can turn to when I have questions about anything related to either cover or interior artwork. Another very patient person who tolerates my many questions.

And finally to the many contributors to this book - the authors and the artists - for your outstanding work. I hope you find this anthology to be the top notch showcase of your work that you deserve it to be.

Photo by John D. Stanton

## Memory to Perish

## by Carmen Tudor

I built my house in the shadows of the Cambrian Mountains. The deep gray-green of the landscape's jagged edges sliced the pure blue of the horizon and then disappeared on hazy summer afternoons or black winter nights like a vision turning to dust. I liked it from the first moment I saw the place. I hadn't been thinking about a lifetime's interment then. I'd been thinking about a year or two of solitude. After some time alone there the colors dulled and bled together, and my eyes saw more than grass and sky. I saw the place as a vision of my own creation, and so too did those vile lawmakers who in time were as happy as I to use the house as something infinitely more than walls of stone.

"They are dead, they shall not live; they are deceased, they shall not rise..." The solitary voice, spoken lowly, reverently, snuffed out the quiet whimpering of Rhys. Not yet having lived his twentieth year played a part, I'm sure, in Rhys's sniveling as he was led alone and unshod toward one of the back doors of the old house. The speaker's voice rose only enough to continue to be heard over the ticking of the mantle clock. His perfect timbre and enunciation lent the occasion a mournful quality as if he were speaking the words of a dirge or requiem. If I allowed myself the thought it was, in fact, more like extreme unction. But he, the speaker, was no man of God. And Rhys was without hope of redemption.

The setting sun glinted off Rhys's stubbled jaw. His hair, cropped short and setting him apart as a man soon to die, was uncommon in these parts. But to me he was a sight only too familiar. They were all brought to me like this: hairless, trousers short like those of a child, and with naked feet that grazed the rough ground with jarring steps.

I let the curtain fall away from my hand and waited for the slide of the bolt in the door of the back kitchens. My ears picked up the low scrape as though standing next to the housekeeper Bronwen and her boiling kettles. I use the plural because as she set the iron pots upon the flames I distinctly recall two clunks. And her thin shoes as they padded across the floor. It was in my nature to observe; it was in my nature to hear.

Soon Rhys's sniveling was in my very house. The biblical verses, so low and somber, followed too and after several minutes a rap on my door settled my thoughts. I straightened my cravat and opened the door. Rhys was even more pitiful up close. A tall young man, he stood well above my height, and lacked nothing in breadth. Errant tears and a streaming nose cast aside handsome features. Sayer stopped his recitations and nudged the boy forward.

"This is him. Papers signed and stamped only last night. Take care, Dafydd. They say he's something of an escapist."

I nodded at Sayer, but kept watch of the boy. He hadn't yet looked up, hadn't met my eyes. After all this time I'd yet to meet one who could. Except Carys. She remained the exception and I knew it was only her brash youthfulness that set her apart.

Sayer nodded back and turned away. His job was done. He would resume his official duties and count his coins without fault or stumble. On Sunday he would take his seat at chapel and cleanse himself from his ills—whatever they might be—and sooner or later there he would be—delivering another baby to Gelert. I wished for the luxury to repent and forget;

my curse, however, was eternal. My curse, as it seemed, was some sort of damnation on earth.

"Rhys."

The boy flinched at his name, his hands at his sides, raw from the fetters.

"Did no one ever teach you to be proud of your name?"

Perhaps he hadn't the head for questions, or perhaps the situation was as horrifying as he'd anticipated. I made no effort to horrify; in fact, I was trying to be pleasant. His weeping ceased.

"Rhys."

This time the boy lifted his head. He met my gaze. Held it.

"That's better." Striding past the youth, I didn't bother to check if he followed or not. I knew he did. Had his footfalls on the carpeted floor not given him away, the knowledge that they always followed rested somewhere at the back of my mind. They couldn't help themselves anymore than I could. They were animals at night—predators and miscreants. But in my presence, they submitted to my will. Had it not been so pathetic I may have laughed.

"Have you ever seen such a house as this?"

There were so few people to talk to that I allowed myself the indulgence of engaging in a mild chatter every so often. Rhys pleased me more than most. His youth, I suppose, was something I couldn't blame him for. If he'd had any hope at all, it was because of his youth.

"It is a fine house, isn't it? I built it stone by stone. This place here will stand long after the very mountains have slipped. It would have made a fine ancestral home and I have no son, of course, but perhaps someday..." I slowed. I wanted Rhys's feet to feel something other than rough earth and splintered

3

flagstone. "This room has seen Gwynedd County's finest ladies and gentlemen. They have danced and drunk the most excellent wines in here. That settle over there rested the weary gentry. Do I bore you, Rhys?"

Turning, I found the boy several paces behind, gazing at a portrait of Carys. The way he appraised her face quickened my pulse. There was a chance he saw something there, the same quality I had seen. I didn't know what Rhys's crimes had been, and I didn't want to know. Unless he had a fondness for children.

"Carys," I said. But, no. Rhys didn't exude the noxious odor of one so inclined. Whatever he had done harmed only himself; he had wronged no one. "The way you stare is as if you know her. She is not your sister?"

Rhys heard me then. He shook his head and dutifully eyed the pretty settle. "It is fine." His monotonous voice was raspy for someone so young. I had forgotten he must have spent the night crying for his life. Youths weren't often sent to me. Some of the elders laughed or spat at my feet, and this is what I had expected of Sayer's latest delivery.

"Would you like to see where the most beautiful flowers and fruits are grown? There are roses of many colors. Oranges and strawberries also."

Rhys licked his lips, but his eyes remained wide. He must've thought I was mad. It humored me somewhat too, so I took no offence.

The conservatory must have assaulted the boy's senses. The warmth and the scents of the plants could be like standing within a dream. He stopped when I stopped. "Go in," I said. Rhys's feet left the carpet and wandered over the flagstone one small step at a time. "You may take an orange if you like. Two, if it pleases you."

4

Rhys's filthy hands reached up and selected just one orange. I watched intently as his face passed a blossom, stopped there a while, and assumed half a smile.

"It is bewitching. But the roses too. You must."

Half an hour later I took a handkerchief from my breast pocket and cleaned my hands. Carys never liked it when I came to her afterward without first cleaning my hands rigorously. The memories it must have caused her pained me. We never spoke of just how close she'd come to succumbing to Sayer's plan.

I found her in her room. She sat at a desk by her window. "Did you give him fruit?" she asked.

I smiled at her as best as I could. "I did."

"And you were kind?"

"I was kind."

"But not as kind as you were to me?"

Her gaze fell on my sharp nails—so claw-like, though she never backed away. She had known Rhys wasn't like the rest. She must have watched his arrival just as I had. She must have heard the cries.

"No. Not as kind as I was to you. You forget what I am, that I am more beast than man."

"I never know when I can believe you or when you are telling a lie." She tried to smile. "It cannot be helped. Can it?"

"No, love. It cannot. I cannot."

"But you could. If you chose."

"No, love. I am what I am, and I do what I do for us so that we may stay. Remember that. Remember it always."

Carys said no more.

As the days and nights passed she displayed a restlessness I had never seen before. When Sayer brought a man to the door, Carys was there. She would wait and watch—no doubt seeking a sign of a being like her. Of a being like Rhys. The young man was in her thoughts often, and in mine as well. I always came to her when the deed had been done and she always looked up into my eyes and begged me to tell her it was over. I would tell her so, but I knew to my core it was not what she meant.

It happened some time later that another youth somehow found his dirty feet standing at my door. Unbound at the hands, but familiarly shackled at the ankles, he broke the skin of his knuckles and palms with his entreaty of entry. I smelled the blood and desperation of his plea. Bronwen came to me and I nodded assent.

In the kitchen the youth shivered next to the stove.

I bared my teeth. "If you only knew to what house you have come."

His nervous gaze flittered to me, and then over my shoulder. Carys stepped past me and into the room. She took in the sad sight of the boy and knelt at his fettered feet. "Dafydd. Help me. We must hide him before they come."

The boy inched away from Carys's touch.

"He will not hurt you," she told him.

"Carys!" She wasn't used to hearing my voice filled with anything but love. The sound of my disapprobation had startled her and she questioned me with a pained look.

"Why ever would you hurt me? I came seeking sanctuary." Neither of us had expected the boy to speak. Although his teeth chattered from the cold, his voice was firm and his gaze steady. Carys ineffectually worked the locks of his shackles. They rattled on the floor between his scratched and frozen feet.

"This is the house," Carys told him. "This is where they were bringing you. You have caused your own death. I cannot help you now." She looked up at me questioningly. Her face held the same innocent look she had bestowed upon me all those years earlier. A look mirrored in the portrait I had seen so many times. It was what stilled my racing heart and maintained my humanity. It was what kept me alive.

"To show mercy to one would spell my end, Carys. You know that."

Taking my arm, she walked out of the room with me. Bronwen sat with the boy. The quick sliver of her knife slicing vegetable peelings was as clear to me, as close, as if I were shaving my cheek. That sound, mingled with the baying of dogs in the distance, was the thing to which I clung.

"Do this, Dafydd. It is all I will ever ask of you." She took my hands in hers and pressed them firmly. "We can leave this place. We'll go where Sayer will never find us, to Cardiff, anywhere. We will start a new life. We will start a new life together, and never speak of this time again."

Carys's bravery in speaking to me so fervently tore my heart—or what of it still remained—in two. I loved her more than ever before for what she offered me: her life for his. But Carys had never been my prisoner and I would not take her as such now. Whatever she was to me—daughter, friend, confidante, companion— she had always had my love. She always would.

"Sayer and his men have arrived," I told her. Her hands slipped from mine. "I must greet them, you see." Carys wept bitterly. She turned away from me in disgust. Turned. And ran back to the kitchen to try again to free the boy of his shackles.

Allowing Sayer into my home was the most distasteful part of my existence. I felt the weight of his conscience even more than that of the brutes who spat at my feet. And his men, who followed him here to this hell, were just as bad as he. Bringing them in was the worst part of my day, but as I had told Carys, it was what allowed me to stay. My familial seat was protected so long as I was of use. My own sins were pardoned.

Afterward, when I had washed all the blood from my hands and the starch of Bronwen's potatoes filled the air with a hazy steam, I went to Carys. I dried the tears from her eyes. "It is time to go," I told her. A spot of blood, small enough that she wouldn't have even felt it fall there, rested on her face. It loosened and swirled with her tears and I hastened to clear it away.

"And what of him?" She pointed to the boy.

"He must go too. It isn't safe for him now."

I took the boy's shackles between my hands and tore the length of chain in two. He balked at my strength but didn't say a word. He, like Carys, had seen what I was. He had heard the cries and witnessed the bloodshed. More than that, he had glimpsed what was to have been his own fate. He and Carys shared that knowledge between them. And I would let them have it.

"Go."

"But, Dafydd—"

I tried out a small smile, just for her. "Your memory shall do me well, cariad bach. Remember that always."

The clock on the mantle ticked its steady rhythm. It too, with its unfeeling beat, contained something of an answering, mournful voice. But it was

8

better than Sayer. It was better than Carys also. It was steadfast. With the winding of a key, it would go on as long as I, the beast of Gwynedd, would. I watched it for some time with the knowledge that it would be enough.

On the eve of what would have been Carys's twenty-fifth birthday I lit a candle. I was slower by that time. Perhaps not in the way others may have sensed, but something like decay had settled over my thoughts and each movement I made lacked the agility I had previously known. As I stood watching the flame burn, the little drops of burning wax landing on my fingers made me smile. The sensation awoke a memory of many years before, when cast from my home I had reveled in the pain of freedom. Although freedom is often cited as costing nothing, I knew there was a very real price to be paid, and it usually involved the spilling of blood.

My freedom, and the scars it had cost, weren't worth much any more. This old house in the shadow of mountains where even the sun struggled to reach really would provide something of an interment. I blew out the candle. Maybe my senses weren't as poor as I had imagined, for the darkness showed a scene to me as clear as any other. After striding through the hall, I found myself standing below the portrait of Carys. It may have done me well to take it down, to carry it with me where I was going. But on second thought, it might have done me no good at all. Although I no longer thought about her, she would occasionally creep into the mists that fell across the door or, as I well knew, into the very darkness of night. I was sure it wasn't my doing. These things, contradictory things not meant to be believed, had a way of grasping on nonetheless. Clawed fingernails

9

weren't necessary. Nor was a drowning desperation. No, I recognized resignation would have the same effect.

The Cambrian Mountains stand as proud as ever. The grass grows green and although the vaults below the house know no difference between green and blue, my own memories of things past will do. If I were a prayerful man I might repent my violent deeds and think back with a hope for redemption. As it stands, the vaults will hold me long before I turn to dust and long before my bones are all that remain.

Illustration by Joshua L. Hood

The Grinning Cat

by Brandon Ketchum

I took delivery of a box containing Dr. Ambrose Henney's personal effects late on the night of his mental breakdown. I had been hard at work, poring over my notes until midnight was but a distant memory. A light rain fell outside the open window of my study, introducing a welcome coolth to the room. The teasing scent of damp pollen wafted to my nostrils, carried on the breeze; now, whenever it rains in the summer, I equate the smell with Henney's queer situation.

An orderly arrived with the doctor's possessions and a short verbal message. The orderly assured me the good doctor had been in control of his teetering wits when he gave over his things. Tired as I was, I felt unequal to the task of going through them. Though I wondered at the orderly's choice of words, I surmised he was being dramatic, and sent him away. I resolved to investigate the matter further after a few hours of slumber.

The first item I noticed atop Dr. Henney's belongings the next morning was a thin book. The rough edges of a poorly folded paper poked out from beneath the cover. I slid this free, carefully unfolding it to discover the hasty scrawl of a letter. So spidery were the words, it was difficult to read Dr. Henney's practiced hand in them. As a proponent and student of Abbé Michon's science of graphology, I was able to confirm it was his writing; the letters still contained a plethora of backward loops. This indicates a man who thinks a lot, and bears great responsibility. These traits described Dr. Henney exactly, and backward loops littered all of his writings.

The letter introduced Dr. Henney's journal. It said, in halting lines, he had suffered grotesque horrors the previous night, and could no longer tolerate the company of society. Dr. Henney was committing himself to Marshalsea Sanatarium, to live out his days tucked away from the many stresses of the world. Marshalsea had been his sanctuary for years, where he practiced psychiatric arts in an attempt to soothe wits and rehabilitate minds. Now it was to be his home, a place so comfortable and familiar, so isolated from external stimuli, so as to keep him from going insane.

It ended by explaining he had remained composed long enough to pen an account of what had happened to him in Bentleyville. He concluded with a desperate hope that, by scribbling his tortures onto the page, he would somehow be able to banish them from his memory, or lessen his mental anguish.

The following is the text of his account.

Frustration ruled my mood that morning. The board of Marshalsea Sanitarium had rejected all my new experimental treatments as unorthodox. I fumed, raging against the small-mindedness of the stuffy old curmudgeons populating the psychiatric profession. Were we destined to be mired in the ignorance of antiquity for all time, to consider in raw wonder the awesome expanse of the human psyche? Or would we doctors forge ahead and, through systematic approaches of trial and error, develop new ways of measuring and studying the inner workings of man's thoughts and dreams?

I was thus in quite the mental lather when I went to see Mr. Patterson. He had been committed to Marshalsea without the capacity for speech. The staff assumed he had suffered some unbearable mental

13

trauma, his body suppressing his voice to protect him from hearing his own tortured ravings. I agreed with the staff. Mr. Patterson's wild eyes and filthy, disheveled appearance lent credence to this theory. We determined he needed to be coaxed back to an acceptance of reality, to overcome his mental block so as to be able to speak again. I took him under my care with the intention of using some of my less objectionable therapies to ease his torment.

I soon had to reassess my opinion. Once we began his standard physical examination, the medical doctor discovered Mr. Patterson's vocal apparatus had been completely neutralized, the chords rendered raw and unusable. As there were no outward signs of trauma, the medical staff determined he had screamed himself past the point of vocal endurance. I found myself vexed, wanting to know what the poor, disturbed man may have seen and experienced to drive him to the brink of insanity.

A few days later, Mr. Patterson regained some of his ability to speak, the swelling in his vocal chords having begun to subside. He could manage only a vague whisper, but I was anxious to attend Mr. Patterson, for my professional curiosity demanded I delve into his psyche and glean what I could about his condition. His case had caught at the edges of my curiosity, and I felt inexplicably drawn to be the first to hear his tale.

When I arrived at his bedside, with Mr. Patterson strapped securely in place as a precaution against self harm, it was clear he was not much in our rational world. He was cognizant of my presence, but his eyes told me he was not whole. He seemed willing to speak, though I had to lean near his mouth in order to piece together his words. Even so, I managed to glean only bits of his speech.

14

"Nighttime by the spring...Bentleyville Pike...organ music...haunting...beautiful...dreadful...follow...cemetery...clearing...too bright...grinning--Oh God, it's still grinning..."

And then, already teetering at the edge of the abyss, Patterson's mind broke, tumbling him into the oblivion of madness. The light of understanding faded from his eyes as he fell comatose.

The following days were little more than a distracting afterthought. I brooded, unable to concentrate on my work. The board's continuing obstreperousness could no longer raise my ire. I drifted through rounds like a pale ghost, visible yet immaterial. A strange notion took seed in my mind, growing over the passing days from barely the hint of a thought to an overbearing desire. Why not investigate this locale in Bentleyville? The Bentleyville Pike bridged the stream Patterson had babbled about, the only stream of note in its environs. The idea made no sense, for Patterson's utterings were probably only mad fantasies, yet it probed the unease in the depths of my being. It was the only way to clear my mind.

I would arrive early in the evening at the scene Patterson had described with the intent to camp beside the spring until dawn. Upon awaking I would investigate the cemetery and see if I could find a clearing nearby. This done, my mind would be able to rest on the topic, and I could focus once more on my important and lately unattended work.

Thus fortified with a plan of action, I tied up all loose ends at work as quickly as possible. I passed off my patients to a colleague that morning, pleading illness, and made for home. Once there, I packed a bedroll and a few modest foodstuffs of cheese, bread,

15

and cold beef. After a hasty luncheon, I saddled my horse and set out.

I had a cheery disposition as I rode the pike that afternoon, free from care. Glad to be out of the stuffy halls of the sanitarium and in the open air, I tilted my cheek up into the sun's warm splendor, the fresh breeze tickling at my ear. The pike was free of mud, so my mount had no trouble with the road. So giddy was I with the sense of adventure and appreciation for the outdoors, I resolved to take such rides more often.

Arriving at a small bridge late in the afternoon, I knew the burbling stream that ran beneath it must be the stream Patterson had rambled about. I turned off the pike and directed my horse along a wide game trail that ran through the forest and paralleled the flowing waters. I rode along cheerfully for some half an hour before I pulled back on the reins. The path diverged from the stream a short way ahead, rising gently onto a small hill. Looking down at the stream I observed a flat, shaded spot on the bank. The place was covered by the foliage of the woods, and sat just beside the stream in the lee of the hill. Grass grew aplenty along the bank, so my horse would be able to graze. A perfect campsite.

After tending to my mount, I set up my bedroll and broke my fast, glorying in the serenity of the forest and the whisper of water over rocks. As I relaxed, leaning against the hill, the evening began to fade into the early reaches of night. A slight chill crept upon me, bringing with it a strange peace, as if I were doing precisely what the universe desired. The moon was out and the night clear, so I disdained lighting a fire. I wrapped myself in a blanket and passed slowly, comfortably, into slumber.

Something disturbed my sleep, and I awoke suddenly in the middle of the night. At first I was at a loss as to why I felt so completely alert when I had just a moment before been sound asleep. Something of cosmic importance was at hand. I felt it in the prickling of the gooseflesh on my arms, and in the electric energy that stood my hackles to attention. I was excited and prepared. Glancing around, I noticed a slight mist lay piecemeal over the stream, outlined in silver by the light of the moon.

It was then I felt a slight pressure on my chest. Turning my head from the stream, and tucking my chin to my chest, I found there a large tabby cat, studying my face with feline piquancy. The tabby meowed, stepped off my body, and sauntered into the woods. I somehow knew I must follow this cat; the answers I sought about Patterson's madness lay at the far end of its path. The horse whinnied, but the sound barely registered, its urgency muted in my mind as I focused on the cat. I pushed the blanket from me and levered to my feet, setting off up the bank and into the forest.

As I began through the woods, I found my way curiously free of underbrush. I was at first afraid I would lose sight of the tabby, but I need not have worried. It seemed every time the cat wound behind a tree and out of my sight, I would rush forward, only to find it looking back and awaiting me on the other side. My being was afire with an indefinable urgency, which eclipsed my previously inquisitive mindset. I felt as if an alien source of intellect had seized control of my imagination, that it was fueling my desire, my now insatiable need, to follow this cat to where it might lead.

By this time we had penetrated far into the wood, and a foreign sound reached my ears. The

17

haunting music just barely tickled my ears, and was as out of place in the wilderness as a woodchuck would have been in a tuxedo. I at first tried to convince myself it was the wind piping through the branches, but as I followed the tabby farther and the sound increased in volume, I could no longer deny I was hearing the echoing chords of an organ. Patterson had been correct.

The cat turned and squinted intently at me, as if to say I had no choice but to continue on. The feline intensity behind those eyes was frightening, but thrilling too, and I no longer had any trepidation about what I was doing. I felt only a desire to continue on.

I was therefore undaunted when the cat led me into an overgrown and abandoned cemetery there amidst the woods. I vaguely recalled hearing the old Bentleyville cemetery had been located in a forest glade. As I stepped between the weathered, vine-enwrapped stones, the organ music increased in volume. It sounded as if I were sitting in the same room as the ghostly organ player. The music had no definable melody, yet it did not fall with discordance upon my ears. It was soothing and teasing at the same time. I stepped through the graveyard and after the still-moving tabby, careful not to trip over the vines, as we paced toward the organ's source.

Beyond the cemetery stood a ring of ancient oak trees. They were enormous, and grew in what looked like a perfect circle, bathed in the scintillating glory of the moon's glow. The sight was so magnificent I slowed to a stop. The music had become so loud as to be almost unbearable, and I was now certain it originated from the middle of this benighted grove, though I could not see its source.

A shrill meow, full of disapproving impatience, snapped me from my awed reverie and back into the moment. The organ was blasting at my ears and the tabby was gazing at me expectantly. With a meek dip of my head, in apology, I strode forward and followed once again.

The tabby sauntered past the bole of one of the looming trunks, leading me amidst the trees. I felt an inner peace, knowing I trod where I was meant to tread, but when I reached the center of the grove my limbs froze, rooting me to the spot. My sense of kismet fled. The cat stopped and looked at me, and I labored to breathe. I wanted to look away from the tabby, but its eyes had locked with mine and I could not break the gaze. The cat grinned, a lazy tugging at the corners of its mouth that bloomed into a hideous, loathsome baring of its teeth. The cat knew. It probed the depths of my soul with its freakish green eyes, memorizing the nightmares of my subconscious being, and grinned. The music jolted to a halt, a blinding flash of light exploded in my eyes, and I fell unconscious.

Much later I returned to my senses. I tried to open my eyes, but the lids were pressed so heavily closed I was unable to will them open. I tried to reach up with my hands to pry them apart but, with a growing sense of panic welling up within my breast, I found I did not have command of my limbs. I could not even open my mouth to cry out in surprise at this supernatural paralysis.

I felt a stabbing pain in my eyelids, as if pins pricked at them, rending through the flesh of my lids. An unbearable luminescence glowed all around, driving through the holes, searing my eyeballs. Yet my eyes came into focus, showing the ring of oaks on the periphery of my sight. The points of light burning into my eyes were the stars, blazing down from the gaping sky. Yet they could not have been the stars, for stars are not so painfully bright. Only what else could they be?

I felt a presence on my chest, and knew it was the creature responsible for my predicament. I still could not move, and I dearly wished to lie there unmolested until morning, when I was sure the tabby would be forced to release me from this nightmare without harm. I endeavored to keep my gaze skyward, but my body was no longer my own. With slow, evil progress, my chin tucked down into my chest, inching my gaze closer to my own body. There on my chest lounged that wicked cat, grinning away at my predicament.

The tabby licked its paws with malicious care, then stood and looked skyward. No matter how I much I hated looking at that devil cat, I did not want to look there again. The cat looked back into my eyes and grinned again. I felt with sickening certainty that what I would see in the sky would end my sanity. As if it were some hellish puppet master, the cat locked my gaze and began to look up at the sky again, and I was forced to move my head and eyes and look at the sky along with it. Immediately I began to gibber in frothing panic, but only in my mind, for I still was not allowed the use of my own voice. And so my mind howled its agony, gripped as it was with wave upon wave of panic.

There in the sky above me, though by all laws of gravity it was beneath me, was the eldritch grove in which I already lay. To my further horror I saw, lying on the ground in the center of the circle, my own self. And on my chest stood a tabby cat, looking skyward at me, its feline mouth twisted in a mocking rictus. At first I thought I was experiencing an out-of-body phenomenon, but my instincts told me it was something far worse. Around my prostrate body in the sky, the grove was crisscrossed with lines, forming a giant pentacle, pushing out and connecting with the base of the trees. This pentacle was an impossibility, the lines not truly lines. They bent in odd directions, neither angular nor circular, certainly not straight. They turned back again into themselves, mocking the science of geometry, forming smaller shapes that bespoke the utter hopelessness of mortal man. But when I took in the pentacle as a whole, and did not look at the distinct parts of the demonic sign, it looked normal enough.

Normal! Nothing within that nightmare picture of darkness was normal. I fretted inside myself, mentally thrashing back and forth against my paralytic bonds. As if to punctuate how supernaturally abnormal the present reality was, a hellish red light began to pulse within the grove, highlighting the pentagram in deepest Cimmerian black each time it flashed. I realized the color was throbbing on and off to the rhythm of the organ music, and the music was twisting into my ears, tickling them in a sickening manner, as if corpses were trying to nuzzle them as a lover would.

These visions, the music, and the awfully grinning cat, they may have driven me mad in that moment. Still I was not allowed the release of screaming. Though it was a wretched situation, I might yet have endured a full return to reality had it ended there. Instead, I was made to behold dirt churning into small mounds within the pentacle, like moles preparing to push free into the open air. These clods of earth heralded nothing quite so mundane as moles, no. I beheld tendrils of white flesh as they wormed their way out of the upturned earth. Yet these were not the fingers of pale human flesh, but the noses of vast maggoty things, the bloated bodies of which thrusted through the final dirty barrier of the ground. These enormous grubs burrowed upwards until the majority of their bloated bodies had won free of the earth, my own most intimate nightmares clawing free of their graves, flopping flat like grotesque fish emerging from brackish water instead of from earth.

I struggled frantically, bucking against my spectral bonds. I was still denied the movement of my own body, but my voice returned. I could finally give voice to my tortured mind. I began to scream then, and did so without cease. They twisted and snaked around and atop each other, and I screamed in the face of the awful knowledge of what they would do next. Though these things had no eyes to see me, nor ears to hear my screams, they instinctually knew where I lay. As I tried and failed to roll to my feet, to flee that grove full of devil-spawned creatures, they wended toward me, onto me, over me. Though I could see none of the maggots around my true body, I could somehow feel what was happening to that other me in that other grove, proving this to be no mere out-of-body experience. Even as they buried me under their sickening weight, they left my eyes uncovered, so I could view it in its entirety. The blackest of my nightmares had come alive to torture me, and as I felt and watched it unfold, I could only scream.

I thought I was broken already, but I was horribly mistaken. My mouth and throat filled with gelatinous tissue as I looked on and watched the slimy blobs in the grove probe my body. This further assault removed from me the ability of speech, but I forced the air up into my voice box. My throat undulated with effort as I continued to scream, unable to unleash my tortured cries into the Stygian night. Nor could I tear my eyes from the sight, for I still could not move. The cat on my chest grinned up at me as I was undone.

I do not know how long I tried to scream, or when the hellish ordeal ended. I remember waking up terrified early the next morning, a few short bits of the headlong flight home along the Bentleyville Pike, and the sudden irrepressible desire to banish myself from society. I yearned to clear my mind of the tabby cat and its awful grin, but I knew I never would. I could barely breathe for the terror of this remembrance. I put pen to paper, but my hands trembled so violently I blotted the page. I crumpled it and drew another sheet, forcing my hands to cease their tremors. I scribbled words in a forced scrawl, my hand cramping with every effort, and I fouled many more as I recorded this heinous memoir. As you read this book, the hell-spawned cat and its awful grin will still be etched upon my mind's eye, and it will resist all attempts to erase it. No one would ever believe what I have written herein, and so I bequeath my awful, nightmarish truths to you, my dearest friend. Keep them close, and for God's sake, keep away from the woods around Bentleyville.

I am thus committing myself to Marshalsea Sanitarium, never to leave. I will huddle within the protective confines of its walls and clutch the shredded remains of my sanity tightly to me until the day I finally, mercifully, die.

Thus ended the puzzling, raving tale contained in Ambrose Henney's journal. The final sentences were so roughly penned it was if I could feel his wits buckling with each word.

23

I am the only man with the ghastly knowledge of why Henney went finally and irrevocably insane, condemned to the hideous mental plateaus of total madness. Whatever truly happened, his experience had battered his sanity so badly he was on the cusp of losing all when he committed himself. And the cruel irony is, his own work finished him. The board, the very morning of his trip, had approved the application of one of his new treatments, and Henney was the first to partake of it. A flood of kittens cascaded into his cell the next day, the same hour I began to read his account, mewling adorably, a litter of rescued tabbies recruited to help soothe the troubled patients.

The Castle at the Edge of the World

by Sheldon Woodbury

There are mysteries within mysteries
worlds within worlds
unknown forces waiting to unfurl
she awoke with a moon lurking and dreary
a haunting orb shining so eerie

Her husband was cloaked as black as a crow
clutching a candle with a sputtering glow
his eyes still shimmered with gloomy delight
on this their sacred wedding night

Please come my love he urged with a swoon
gazing out at the lurking moon
she slipped out of bed with a stumbling chill
the shadowy room silent and still

It felt like a dream as they descended down
the echoing stairs to the outside grounds
my beloved she implored where are we going
the dread in her heart suddenly growing

A ghost like mist clawed at the towers
a macabre sight at this midnight hour
the ocean thrashed with watery growls
like a giant behemoth beginning to howl

They appeared from some unknown beyond
where all our mysteries are secretly spawned
the lurking moon became a monstrous eye
a horrifying sight in the midnight sky

Good-by my love her husband whispered

clutching her hand with a trembling shiver
there are mysteries within mysteries
worlds within worlds
unknown forces waiting to unfurl

Photo by John D. Stanton

## The Governess

### by Misha Herwin

My footsteps echoed along the empty street. The fog that had hung over the city since daybreak had grown thicker. A grey blanket of hopelessness, it pressed around me, deadening familiar sounds, distorting shapes, so that buildings loomed up unexpectedly and streets stretched into invisible distances. I had been walking for hours and now I no longer knew where I was. There was no friendly face to ask the way. Only those whose business had to be attended to under cover of darkness would venture out on a night like this. But I had no choice.

I clutched the strings of my reticule, afraid that it might be snatched by some pickpocket lurking in the impenetrable gloom. It contained all the money I had left in the world and the address of the house I was looking for. It had to be close, but how could I tell? Shrouded by fog the thin tall houses looked alike. My stomach twisted with unease. Being unfamiliar with the city, I was already late. If I did not arrive soon, would they turn me out, throw me onto the streets, back to the cold hearted charity of my stepmother?

Some distance ahead a gas lamp threw a ray of sulfurous light through the darkness. I hurried towards it, hoping to get my bearings and a shadow flared out onto the pavement. I stopped. I glanced around me. Nothing moved and through the eerie silence all I could hear was the pounding of my own heart. Summoning up what little courage I had, I stepped into the lamplight and saw beside it the street sign I had been looking for.

The windows of number twenty Belvedere Terrace were blank. Had they forgotten I was coming? What would I do? Where would I go, if they had? My hand trembled as I lifted the doorknocker. It fell with a cold hard thud. I waited but no one came. I hesitated, afraid to knock again in case I appeared rude and impatient, after all this house was my only hope. I knocked again and, to my relief, heard the sound of bolts being drawn.

The front door opened into a narrow hall. Flickering gaslights threw a pall over the dark green wallpaper and black and white tiled floor. A stale unused smell hung in the air as if this house did not welcome visitors. I drew in my breath and stepped inside.

"Follow me, miss," the housemaid said. "We've been waiting for you." My heart jumped into my throat. After all the uncertainty of the previous days, was I finally going to meet my mysterious employer? The maid, however, was opening the door to the servants' staircase.

"Mrs. James, the housekeeper, says I am to take you to her sitting room," she said clattering down the wooden stairs. I was to be treated like one of the servants. This was not what I had expected when I accepted the position. My own governess had been treated as one of the family and this I confess is what I had hoped for. The housekeeper's sitting room was warm and cozy with a good fire in the hearth and at the sight of the tea things laid out on a small side table my spirits lifted.

"My dear, you are very late." Mrs. James rose from her chair. "I was expecting you a while ago. I am afraid you must leave at once."

My head spun and I put out my hand to steady myself. Was she dismissing me? Had I already been

29

found wanting? Was rejection to be the pattern of my life from now on?

The housekeeper glanced at the clock on the mantelpiece. "You are to fetch the child from Temple Meads Station. The train is due to arrive at nine o'clock." Was there a hint of embarrassment in her voice? I had been offered neither tea nor any other refreshment and now it appeared I would be sent out into the night. And what a night it was.

A grey miasma coiled up from the river, its tentacles reaching into every nook and cranny. The city air, thick with the smoke of a thousand chimneys, the reek of horse dung and the fumes of tobacco that clung round the factories, choked the lungs. No one able to remain safe and warm by the fireside would venture out on a night like this.

A hired cab waited at the front steps. I was bundled inside and we set off down the hill

In spite of my resolution to be brave and to face my new life with courage, my thoughts turned to my situation. With the death of my father, I was totally alone in the world. Believing in the goodness of his second wife, he had made no provision for me. As soon as the funeral was over my stepmother told me she had found me a position as governess and companion to a nine year old girl. I was to leave immediately and never to darken her doors again.

I had always thought myself loved and cherished, all the more so when my stepmother's son came to live with us. He, like me, was a beloved only child. He loved nature and we spent many happy hours playing in the grounds of our family home. We climbed trees, turning the swaying branches into the deck of a sailing ship and heading for the Indies in search of treasure. In the winter we turned these adventures into stories, writing them down in tiny notebooks. As we grew older our feelings changed. A touch of his hand would send my heart racing and when he kissed me and told me he loved me, I knew that we were destined to be together. We planned our future, but it was not to be. Tears rose to my eyes and I had to damp down a sudden pang of longing. It took a few moments, but I succeeded.

There was to be no place for weakness in my new life, if my lover had not been strong enough to stand up for me, then I must do it for myself. To stop myself from sinking into useless self-pity, I concentrated on what I knew about the child I had been sent to meet. Like me, she had recently lost a parent. Her mother had died after a long illness. She had been sent to the seaside in the hope of a cure and the child had gone with her. Was it to give her mother solace in her last months, or to strength the child's lungs in the sea air? Whatever the reason, now that her mother was gone, the little girl was coming home to her grieving father.

I resolved to treat her gently and, since we shared sad histories, hoped that we may in time grow fond of each other, becoming more like sisters than teacher and pupil. The cabby's voice announcing our arrival broke through my thoughts. He helped me down and I hurried through the cathedral-like entrance.

Platforms stretched into the mist and I looked longingly toward the waiting room where a warm fire would be burning. As I did so, I heard the first sound of the approaching train. There were only minutes to wait, then like a creature of nightmare, veiled in clouds of smoke and steam, eyes glowing red, it drew in. Doors banged open. Porters came running to take up the passengers' luggage, then stepped back disappointed as no travelers alighted.

I peered anxiously through the dim light. This was my first task and I had failed my employer. As I stood wondering whether I should return to Belvedere Terrace, two shadowy figures stepped out of the mist. As they came closer, I saw that one was a tall thin man dressed in black. His face white and gaunt, he gripped the hand of a small child as he pulled her along as if she were nothing more than a toy. Like her companion she was dressed in mourning and the cascade of golden hair falling down her back contrasted vividly with the drabness of her cloak and bonnet. Her face was strained, her mouth tight as if holding back any word or cry that might rise to her lips, her eyes shadowed and blank as if she were still in the thrall of some deep and terrible shock.

She stood mutely to one side as I hurried forward to introduce myself. Her companion nodded shortly, then bent his head and addressed the child.

"It was your mamma's final wish that I should bring you here. Now that I have done so, I bid you farewell." Without another word, he walked away. Not once did he look back at the child he had abandoned and my heart went out to the poor little thing. She needed my care more than I had imagined. How must she feel, to be left so abruptly with a stranger?

"Don't be afraid," I said and held out my hand. She said nothing. Swaying slightly on her feet, she looked as if she might collapse at any moment. "What you need is some hot milk and a warm bed. Come." I led her to the waiting cab. Her hand was limp and cold in mine. She did not pull away, but walked stiffly beside me.

Once inside the vehicle, I went to put my arm around her, but when I touched her, she cowered away, tucking herself up in the furthest corner of the seat and I have to admit some of my sympathy

drained away. I told myself she was tired after her
long journey and perhaps like me she had had to learn
to keep her feelings to herself. A good night's sleep
and in the morning, when she was thoroughly rested,
I would see a more pliable and open side to her
character.

Not a single light burned in the windows when
we arrived. There was no sign of the girl's father; the
only person to greet us was the housekeeper.

"Oh my little darling," she cried bending down
to look at the child. "How cold you are and how weary
you must be after all your travels. Let me take your
cloak and bonnet. There's a fire in your room and I'll
be bringing up some supper shortly." With a groan,
she heaved herself to her feet. "He won't see her. Not
tonight," she muttered with a sideways glance at the
child. I nodded. I was uneasy at this turn of events,
but it was not my place to comment. I hoped there
were good reasons for the master's behavior. A child
who had lost her mother needed the love of her father
and to come home to such a cold welcome was hard
indeed. My own father would have taken me on his
knee and held me and comforted me, but perhaps my
employer was a recluse who scorned human company,
or was so overcome by his recent loss that he wished
to hide himself away with his sorrow.

"I've put her in the nursery," Mrs. James
continued. "You are to have the nanny's room. Your
luggage has been taken up." There was no word about
whether I would be comfortable or not, but that was
my new situation in life and I swallowed down my
hurt and resentment as I followed the housekeeper
upstairs. The child trailed behind us, her steps
growing heavier as we reached the final flight.

"It will be good to be back in your old nursery,
will it not?" I asked, hoping to encourage her, but

there was no reply. Hanging her head, she toiled onward. When the housekeeper opened the door and motioned us forward, the child lingered on the threshold.

I was longing to remove my cloak and bonnet, unpack my things and have a moment or two to myself, but I bit back my impatience. As far as I could see, there was nothing about the room to cause my charge such disquiet. It was clean and airy with a good fire in the hearth. The bed was made and there was fresh water and a clean towel on the washstand. There were no toys or pictures on the walls, but cleanliness and order are of the first importance and perhaps her more personal possessions would be in her luggage.

"I will send up some bread and milk and a pot of tea for you," Mrs. James said.

"Thank you." I nodded at my charge to prompt her response. It did not come and it occurred to me that perhaps all the secrecy and haste that had surrounded her arrival were because she was simple minded. That too would explain why her father did not want to see her. But if it were true, what was my role? I had no experience with young children and certainly not with any such as this. On the other hand, if I were to complain and lose my position I had nowhere else to go. I must therefore make the best of it.

There was a flurry at the door and two servants came in carrying a trunk. The housekeeper pointed to the place she wanted them to leave it, but it was the child who spoke.

"I would like my supper now."

"And so you shall," I cried, relieved my worst fears had come to nothing for her voice was clear and she was making good sense. It was the last thing she said that evening, however, and when she had been

34

put to bed she lay beneath the coverlet, her arms folded over her breast, staring open eyed at the ceiling as if the very soul had fled from her body leaving only the husk.

I too could not sleep. Exhausted though I was, I tossed and turned. There was something about this house, the child, the master I had not seen that left me wary and on edge. At last unable to stand it any longer, I got up, thinking to read or maybe write in my journal. The grandfather clock in the hall far below struck midnight. My room was cold, but through the half-open door I saw the last glimmers of the fire in the nursery. Thinking I could warm myself and see to my charge at the same time I threw a shawl around my shoulders and went in.

The bed was empty. The door to the landing open. Beyond it, darkness gaped. A deep and enveloping blackness that drew and repelled me at the same time. I seized a candle and thrust it into the dying embers. The wick caught and holding it high I stepped out into the corridor. My shadow leapt and loomed above me. Candlelight flickered, catching the glass mantles of the gas lamps, the smooth surface of the banister rail, and in the hallway below a white flutter of cotton and lace.

The child stood at the drawing room door. As I hurried down the stairs, her hair glinted in the light of my candle, but her face was white as death, the eyes unseeing. I shuddered. I told myself she was only walking in her sleep, that there was nothing to be afraid of and yet there was something in her stance that was beyond any explanation.

She did not lift a hand, but the door swung open. The room beyond was bathed in a warm, golden glow. A fire blazed in the hearth. Candles burned on the mantelpiece, their light reflected in the mirror

35

above it. There was a faint perfume of roses in the air. A woman sat on a low chair, her fingers twisting in the folds of her blue dress. A man in a frock coat, face thunderous, lips drawn into a narrow line loomed over her. He muttered something and she flinched, then looking up she saw the child. Her face lit up. She rose to her feet, forcing the man to step back as she stretched out her arms. The child ran to her. She caught her hand and they looked up at the man, who raised his fist.

"Stop," I cried as a nameless fear swept over me. I could scarcely move, but knowing I could not leave a child in such a place I made myself enter. One moment there was light, a mother shielding her child, a man suffused with fury, then as swiftly as a breath of wind darkness descended.

My wavering candle lit the shadowy spaces. I saw nothing but heavy old furniture, an empty grate. The cold mustiness of a room long unused closed around me. I called her name; I searched, but there was no sign of the child.

Hoping we had somehow missed each other, I started back up the stairs. My hand gripping the bannister. The rail was slick with sweat, my legs so heavy I had to force myself upward. As I neared the first floor, a door opened and closed. Bunching up my skirts, afraid I may be seen and questioned, I raced up the final flights to the attic. At the nursery door, I hesitated, afraid of what I might see. Was there something I should have done to protect my charge? Or was I too late? Had the mother reclaimed her child?

It took all my courage to enter. The child lay in her bed, still as a statue on a tomb. My heart lurched. On leaden feet I approached the bed, I looked for the rise and fall of her chest. Nothing. Trembling in every limb, fearful for her and for myself, I held my hand above her mouth and finally, between my fingers, I felt the soft in drawing of breath. Clutching at the bedpost, I almost sank to the ground. All was well. Had I dreamed what I had just seen? Was it my grief-stricken and disordered mind that had conjured those images?

I crept into my room and eventually fell into a fitful sleep. The scream woke me. It chilled my blood and set my heart thudding violently. I lay unable to move, fearing for the child and for myself until at last I heard footsteps running up and down the stairs. There was the sound of servants' voices, then the housekeeper saying the doctor must be called for.

The child still slept but I had to know what had happened. I dressed as fast as my trembling fingers would allow and hurried downstairs.

"Oh miss it was awful, his face all twisted and strange," the housemaid wept.

"A sudden seizure," Mrs. James said shortly. "The doctor will confirm it."

"No less than he deserves," the cook said. "Anyone who--"

"That's enough," the housekeeper stopped her with a look. "The master is dead and that is that."

"He never got to see his child," the words came unbidden to my lips. As soon as I had spoken, I knew I should have kept silent. Mrs. James's face darkened.

"Get on your feet and brew a pot of tea," she told the sobbing maid. "There will be no idle gossip in this house," she added with a telling glance in my direction.

At that moment, the kitchen door burst open and the child ran in. Gone was the waif of the night before with her sunken face and withdrawn expression. Plump and merry as if she had been on a

country holiday, her cheeks were flushed, her eyes
sparkled and she fairly danced around the room. So
different was she from the being I had brought home
from the station that for a moment I could not bring
myself to speak, but a glance from the housekeeper
told me I must not shirk my duty.

"Come to me," I said as gently as I could. "It's
all right. I am not angry, but something very sad has
happened." I took her hands and I knelt before her.
"Your Papa," I began, the tears rising in my eyes at the
thought of this new sorrow she must bear as I told her
that her father had died in the night. "I am so sorry,"
I went on, when she did not respond. The silence
stretched between us, then she looked at me and there
was something in those eyes as strange and
unfathomable as death itself. She smiled.

The House of Wellington

by David Schütz II

I

Gazing down from ornate Parapet,
Seth Wellington didst look 'pon Cornish Land.
Land's end and brutal, jagged Shore were met;
The Sea, the Land, the moors were all at hand.
Katherine Wellington to Seth was Wife.
'Twas a union fraught with loathsome Dread;
In turns, there was brief Light, Lament and
     Strife.
A half-score passed and poor Kath'rine was
     dead.
Son William was thus render'd unmother'd,
In slumber didst he walk upon the moors.
'Midst crashing Waves was Katherine found
     smother'd.
Thenceforth her spectral Form didst stalk the
     Shores.
Tyme, like a Cloak, doth cling 'pon Hearts of
     Men;
So Katherine doth plague Seth Wellington.


II

The Moon didst glow'r on House Wellington;
That Castle rose like flames into the Night.
Seth mourned the Years, and raised motherless
     son;
William wouldst oft with his father fight.
The Halls were laden with bleak Woe and Dust,
Echo'd steps didst radiate the Floors.

39

Wounds of the Soul doth make Emotions rust;
Dark permeated Land and Sea and moors.
Katherine didst still walk House Wellington,
Seth turned about at Night 'midst awful
    Dreams.
Dead Mother didst oft sit with maudlin son,
Showing how his father choked her Screams.
In torment breathes the Life that's etched in
    Sadness;
Poor William's Mind and Heart didst wane in
    Madness.

III

Son Wellington into the Years didst walk,
Somnambulant that nightly strode the moors.
The Moon doth clothe the Night in Pitch and
    Chalk;
William's grey Heart clos'd its dark Chambre
    Doors.
Katherine pour'd Vengeance 'to his Ear,
His Vessel filled most loathingly with Hate.
A vile Uxoricide didst slay his Fear;
A bloody Patricide didst seal his Fate.
Across yon Parapet trod Will his Path,
And like the Night, invaded Seth's dark Room.
Opened his father's Throat with sharpened
    Wrath;
Seth Wellington's Bedchambre 'came his
    Tomb.
Within the Night, son's mother's Hand took
    his;
Vanished they in Cornish Sea's Abyss.

Photo by John D. Stanton

## The Revenant of Shelby House

### by Dona Fox

A chill gust of wind snatched the flame from his candle. The narrow tunnel beneath the garden turned as black as Aunt Esther's sable cloak. Edward was trapped in the dark underground labyrinth between Shelby House and the chapel.

Someone, or something, had opened a door at one end of the maze and let in the icy huff of air that blew out the candle. He waited; he would be brave, he would be quiet.

He held his breath and listened, but no door shut; no footsteps echoed in the tunnels. Then he heard it, faint at first, a rattling, like bare bones shuddering together. The sound teased the tender young hairs on the nape of Edward's neck. His belly was tight; his breath was shallow—slow and quiet.

All of Shelby House was darkened for the séance tonight. Skeletons from the family graveyard behind the chapel might be restless. Aunt Esther may have called up a body by the power of the séance Edward had just escaped.

Edward's father said Uncle John and his wife Esther were spiritualists—they traveled the world searching for a secret. Together they tried and tested, every method, every means—to find that secret—the secret to eternal life. As cover for their experiments they tended to the family chapel and the graveyard.

Esther's sister and her husband were here tonight with their twins. Edward's widowed father, George, was also at the séance, and though he was a mortician and an outdoor man who scoffed at spirituality, tonight's séance was being held to contact his wife, Edward's mother.

Edward didn't want to see a dead mother he had never known. That's why he snuck down to the basement, crawled into the bottom of the butler's lift, slid aside the hidden panel, and went into the underground passages.

He wanted to find his way to the chapel then out to the cliffs where he liked to listen to the dark night ocean.

He closed his eyes against the darkness. He dug his nails into the earthen wall; he pressed against the dampness of the underground warren as the clacking grew clearer and louder.

"I see you."

Edward opened his eyes.

The boy was just a bit younger than Edward. He clutched a bare candle in one pudgy hand and a puppet-like figure made up of a number of small pieces of wood tied together with string hung loosely from his other hand.

"What's that?" Edward indicated the figure.

"It's a Limber Guy." The boy looked around the muddy floor of the tunnel, "Is there somewhere I can sit down? I could show you how it works."

"Sure, follow me," Edward surprised himself at how quickly he was able to defeat the maze and locate the chapel with this boy in tow.

The chapel was prepared for a burial the next day. Incense filled the air. Heavily scented flowers to mask the smell of the deceased circled the altar.

Edward used the boy's candle to light the thicker candles placed at the head and foot of the rectangular altar where his uncle laid out the dead for final viewing. He smiled as he sat down and watched the boy pull a narrow board out of his jacket.

The boy perched on the edge of the stone altar, pushed the board part way under his thigh so it stuck out into the air, then he held the Limber Guy just above. He gave the board a flip so it hit the bottom of the puppet's feet and the puppet began to dance. Both boys laughed. After a few dances the boy let Edward try it. Edward made the Limber Guy dance over and over again.

When he turned to tell the boy they should go back to the house, the boy was sleeping peacefully on the altar, surrounded by flowers. The golden glow of the candlelight flickered on his soft young face. The boy had one hand stretched out, his fingers barely touched Edward. Edward hated to wake him, he just wanted to watch him, but he didn't know why.

Hugh found himself amongst the boxes and crates in the freight cars, out of shame, perhaps, but the soot overcame him and he realized how childish that was. At the next stop, he went to the passenger car. He was confused and embarrassed. He couldn't look his travelling companion directly in the eye.

He hid his trembling fists in the pockets of his suit coat. He tried to convince himself it was merely the soot of the train that burned his eyes and caused the tears threatening to seep from the corners of his tightly shut lids.

He loosened his scarves from his collar; they were chafing his neck. He told himself it was simply the excessive warmth of his best woolen suit combined with the heat of the closed private compartment that brought the familiar blush to his cheeks as he remembered the last happy moments of his twenty-two years. Those few moments before the worst humiliation of his life.

Buoyed with the joy of first love, his innocence was not yet shattered as he raced to the gazebo with

the vellum envelope for his twin sister Lilly. He barely
gave a thought to the return address. He knew that
Ned was already in the gardens, waiting for him; Lilly
had gone in place of him to explain that Hugh couldn't
get away today, he had to study.

But delivering the letter to Lilly was all the
excuse he needed to drop those studies and rush to
see Ned, if only for a moment.

He found them deep in the garden, hidden in
the shade of the gazebo. They were on a bench, behind
an ornamental orange tree. Lilly and Ned. Ned's face
was buried in Lilly's bodice and something atrocious
was happening beneath Lilly's skirts for she writhed
on Ned's lap.

Ned didn't see him; Ned's eyes were covered by
Lilly's lace. Lilly didn't see him; her head was thrown
back and her eyes were shut. All summer Hugh had
believed Ned visited to see him—and that Lilly was just
an excuse.

Hugh backed out of the gazebo and hid behind
the fountain. He wanted to flee but, god, he couldn't
stop watching.

After all the months of studying Ned's lips,
feeling the warmth of Ned's breath on his face...all the
days of touching and being touched by Ned's hands,
Ned's palms on his flesh, fingertips brushing his
skin...all the hours and hours of flirting and
innuendos, as they sat close in the garden and talked—
Hugh's emotions were at a fever pitch.

He had seen Ned harden beneath his linen
trousers; he had felt him as they wrestled on the
summer grass. He had thought he was the cause—but
oh, yes, he had not realized—Lilly was there also.

Would he see more of Ned when Lilly took her
satin skirts away? His body burned red with shame
and guilt. But, oh, how he wished he were Lilly.

45

His tears flowed at the loss of his love—his imaginary love.

Everything fell apart. He was so confused.

There was Lilly, her face dead white.

"Hugh. No. Wait. It was a mistake."

He ran. She caught him. They fell to the grass. She held him, they held each other—sobbing.

He couldn't look at her.

"Don't tell. Please don't tell." He could smell Ned on her.

"Let me go, just let me go," Hugh cast her off, somewhat more roughly than he had ever treated her before.

He ran off as she reached out, crying, from the lawn.

Ned left. Hugh had a vision of Lilly, disheveled, running to the train station, crying, beating on the train as it pulled away. Ned, looking straight ahead as if he did not see her, or did not care.

The bastard. The cold-hearted bastard.

Lilly took to her bed in black moiré silk and lace, her hair tied in dark ribbons. A bout of melancholia? She even covered her mirror in black. Had she lost a babe? Hugh was so confused. Lilly was pale and drawn. She caused her room to be filled with flowers. Hugh kissed her lips; she was yet warm.

Why had Ned, who had never loved him, so coldly left his sister too?

The train swerved around a bend; Hugh was thrown against the window. He peeked out of his watery eyes at the man who shared the compartment, his traveling companion, Edward Shelby.

Edward Shelby blushed and looked out the window. Hugh was taken aback. Edward Shelby didn't look like a man who blushed; had he read Hugh's thoughts? Hugh was even more embarrassed.

Edward Shelby, fully decked out in spats and gloves, a smart black tweed suit and gold pocket watch; bowler hat set neatly on his dark curls. He was so formal, yet young enough to be clean-shaven.

Edward Shelby gave off an energy that made Hugh feel alive–drawn to Edward yet strangely nervous. If Hugh looked up he was caught by Edward's eyes. He vowed not to look up again. He kept his hands folded across his chest and his eyes closed for the rest of the journey.

Edward's father, George, in fairly similar attire as Edward, but with a greying beard, met them at the station. Hugh listened to their conversation but neither father nor son addressed their remarks to him so he remained quiet.

"I am glad you are home, Edward. We need to take care of Esther. She still refuses to leave Shelby House," George said.

"Why do we let her stay there, Father?"

"Esther was married to my brother John. You know it is our family duty to take care of her, but I'm concerned about her health. And her sanity. That's why I wrote the letter from Aunt Esther summoning Lilly to join her at Shelby House to fulfill her duty as a loving niece–to be a selfless companion to her dear Auntie in her final years." George kept his eyes on the road.

"You sent the letter, Father? You signed Esther's name?"

"Of course I did. And maybe Lilly could have helped us get that stubborn woman out of Shelby House," George cut off Edward's questions, "We need to hurry. I brought the open carriage and those clouds are full of storm."

Hugh was still so confused. He never gave that letter to Lilly. That letter had summoned him—not Lilly. A forged letter? Had this man's father forged a signature on the letter that had brought him here? Why? Had someone gone insane?

Hugh's questions were forgotten at his first sight of Shelby House.

Hugh paused on the verge, overwhelmed by the perfume of gardenias, jasmine, and roses. Suddenly elated, he wondered how it was possible that such a variety of flowers bloomed in one place.

Mixed with that sublime passion was a feeling he had been here before. He turned to Edward Shelby and all his emotions coalesced; there was something he could not consciously grasp before it drifted away, a feather on the wind.

He turned back to the house and surveyed the gracious Queen Anne mansion before him. Shelby House was the most magnificent home he had ever seen; lights glowed from every window.

The house appeared to be three stories, but with a fourth story tower room. Behind the tower was a balustrade that indicated a large balcony; there were also smaller balconies, outside every upper window, and a porch across the front with substantial well-formed columns.

Hugh saw the whole façade as asymmetrical in a pleasing fashion. Arched window crowns embellished with clam shells, and the usual pendants and brackets were just a few of the Italianate flourishes that he found pleasing.

Looking up so long was beginning to hurt—his neck was stiff and sore from the rough train ride.

Scarlet camellias bloomed on each side of the steps up to the porch; white calla lilies nestled next to the house and ivy trailed down to the carriage path. Eucalyptus scented the air along with salt spray from the nearby ocean.

"Is that a monkey puzzle tree?" Hugh exclaimed as he smiled for the first time in weeks.

"What are you doing here?" A woman's voice called from the front door.

"We've come to help you." Hugh was pleased at the gentle tone in Edward's voice.

"I don't need any help. Go away."

Hugh watched as Edward waved a hand toward the road, "We've brought your nephew, Hugh. We need to get him inside; there's a storm coming."

"I don't need to see him. I never knew him. Take him away."

"Hello, Aunt Esther." Hugh ran up the steps and onto the porch. "A white cat!" Hugh stepped into the house and ran after the cat.

"Stay off my porch." Aunt Esther opened the screen door and stepped out as a gust of air blew in, "I don't have a cat."

A strange spiral of wind blew the door—and the screen door—suddenly shut behind her.

She cringed as George and his son dodged up onto the porch.

George's face was too close, he seemed to babble at her through a haze, "Please, don't be stubborn, Esther. You will be well taken care of now. Help me with her, Edward. Help me get her in the carriage."

Esther struggled against the men as Edward and his father wrestled her into the carriage.

"Did I hear you speak of a white cat?" Edward turned his handsome profile to her for a moment, then, not receiving an answer, he turned his face back to the road.

"Not a white cat, no, a white cat means death," Esther murmured as she gave up. The carriage pulled away. She watched helplessly as her beautiful mansion turned into something ugly and grey as it disappeared in the ocean mist.

Hugh heard Aunt Esther cry out, "No!"

He thought they would take care of her, he needed to stay here and take care of her cat—if only he could find it. He heard something. The cries sounded more like a man weeping in sorrow. Or a soul moaning. He just wasn't used to the house, that was all. He would find the cat. He would feed the cat.

He would run out and tell them that's what he was going to do. Then his sleeve caught on the door frame—his best woolen suit. He extricated the woolen fabric carefully then ran toward the door again only to trip on an uneven board in the floor. Odd, it seemed as if he were wearing thin cloth shoes. But it was winter, and he wouldn't wear canvas spats with a woolen suit. He was so confused.

He got up slowly, he could see them through the window loading Aunt Esther into the carriage; it almost looked as if she struggled against them.

Hugh grabbed the door knob. It was as if jelly were on his hand. He could not get a grip on the knob. He watched helplessly as Edward and George drove off. Edward cast an odd glance at him.

He put his palms to the window and watched as Aunt Esther looked back at the house. Then the carriage disappeared into the fog. Oh, well, he would take care of the cat—and explore the house.

50

In every room keys turned pipes open to allow gas into the wall lamps. The woodwork throughout the house and in the heavy furniture was dark and rich. Multi-colored stained glass windows strained the afternoon light into the house and onto the Persian carpets. Vases of fresh-cut flowers occupied every spot that wasn't already covered.

Hugh looked out the window at the gardens. They were orderly and neat. Much more so than the gardens at home. He blushed at the thought of home and his last disturbing memory of those gardens.

The house was familiar, yet unsettling. One feature that bothered Hugh about the house was the occasional animal trophy on the wall. He had never cared for such trophies and the mounted game in Shelby House seemed permeated with the panic of the animal in the moment before death.

Hugh remembered old terrors from his childhood—how on the nights of the séances at Shelby House, the eyes of the animals glowed in the candlelight. Hugh had imagined each trophy filled with lost souls. He believed they were angry spirits—and they watched him. That's why, when his parents forced him to come to the séances, he preferred to roam the dark underground passages where there were no eyes.

The underground passages that led to the chapel. No. He was not ready to go to the chapel. Not the chapel. He wanted to stay in Shelby House for the moment so he turned instead to the stairs that led to the tower.

Hugh's trepidations-and the white cat-were nearly forgotten when he found the sumptuous burgundy bedroom in the tower. The nest was heavily draped with velvets and silks and piled with half a dozen pillows. He yearned to slip between the sheets and sip the hot chocolate that was yet steaming beside the bed.

But whose bed was this? Whose cup still warm? His heart tightened. Was that a footstep that sounded on the stairs? Was he about to be discovered? He tipped his head to the side and listened. The night was silent but he spied an object lying on the pillows. It was the Limber Guy. The old toy he'd left in the chapel so long ago.

He smiled as he remembered that night. The Limber Guy was a sign, the room had been prepared for him. He clasped the old toy to his chest and, as he sipped the chocolate, he realized how weary he was from the trip. He succumbed to the house completely as he slipped between the satin sheets.

He fell asleep wondering why his neck was still hurting from the train ride.

Edward thought he had seen a pale face at the window, inside the house.

Esther was a bit peculiar. She might not have told them if she had a guest. But did she have a guest or an interloper?

He couldn't leave anyone alone in such a tumbledown ruin—he was going back to make sure there was no one there.

The storm that had held off suddenly came on full force. Edward took the shortcut through the fields in a steady downpour. The water ran in rivulets down his face despite the hood on his whale oil soaked coat.

By the time he arrived at Shelby House, his damp curls lay plastered to his forehead.

The house was set back from the carriage lane, behind arbors covered with vines and dark, molding leaves. Shingles from the roof were scattered around the yard, the oil cloth covering the windows was torn, and the front door stood slightly ajar.

He walked through a series of puddles to the back of the house.

There was no back door, merely a chiffonade of weather distressed oil cloth—now ragged fingers beckoning in the wind. He looked around the back yard and, seeing only the huge dark shapes of the overgrown shrubs, and the crosses and tombstones of the family graves in the distance, he took a deep breath and ducked inside.

No candle light, no gas lamps—open front door, maybe an intruder—Edward chose not to call out.

Wishing he had thought to bring a lantern, he stayed to the right wall as he felt his way cautiously through the house. Maybe darkness would be his friend.

He came to the stairs and he took them. Edward felt a breeze. A door, or a window, had opened.

"Who's there? Hello?" A young man's voice called above the noise of the wind and rain.

Edward's leg went through a rotted floorboard. Reaching out for purchase, he felt a slippery mass on the floor—a body. Straining, digging his fingers into the mushy, pulpy body, he pulled his leg out of the hole in the floor, drug himself across the body, and got to his feet.

A break in the clouds shone moonlight through a broken window as Uncle John rose from the floor. Edward saw Uncle John's unbearably crushed face— his stomach twisted in a mixture of panic, pity and disgust. Uncle John laughed and reached for Edward. Wings fluttered and slapped at Edward's face. Birds. He spun. He threw his arms wildly about.

"We're going to climb the Alps someday, Son."
George threw a pile of ropes and wooden spikes onto
the parlor floor.

Edward spun the piano seat around. "Why,
Father?"

"Because we're men, Edward, we conquer
heights; we're Englishmen, we will take the world one
mountain at a time."

Edward laughed.

"We're going to start with the cliff by the ocean
at Shelby House. I've found a steep, solid rock face-
your Uncle John will join us. He won't say no; if I'm
man enough to do it, he will also."

The night before the climb raced through
Edward's mind in a jumble of fading images that he
pushed away. Buried deep. Denied.

Of course he'd been nervous about the climb.
He couldn't sleep.

Someone crept into his bed. In the dark.

And pierced him. And pierced him again. With
a point, like the point of a sea bird's beak. That's what
he remembered—all he remembered.

He screamed into the darkness.

Father jumped in.

Rescued him.

George rescued his son from the intruder, just
in time. Just barely in time. Edward lay the rest of the
night in shock. Grateful to his father. Forever grateful
to his father for rescuing him. Intent on denial—even
to himself.

There'd been another man in his bed. Deny.
Deny. Deny.

Then Edward was on the cliff face. He could
smell the heat. He could see the salt spray that coated
his arms and he could taste the salt on his lips.

He risked a peek out at the water; bits of sun clung to the points of the waves like diamonds. Then he looked down, straight down to the jagged rocks below and his stomach clenched. He became super-conscious of his position, one hand straining to hold the rope, one foot on the wooden spike below.

His father and uncle had argued. His uncle had wanted to put rings in the rock wall between each climber so that no one of them was dependent on the other; if one slipped or fell it would not impact the others, and the ring would serve as a back up to catch the one who slipped. George didn't understand.

John finally gave in. They had climbed George's way before, they would just have to be careful, as they always had.

George's way was for all three climbers to be roped together with the rope looped around each climber's waist. Supposedly, the strong could support the weak. George put Edward in the middle so they could watch out for him.

Edward was being focused, meticulous and thoughtful in his every move, recalling each procedure his father had taught him before he brought Edward out to the cliff. But suddenly sea birds were screaming and flying at them—attacking them.

Blood covered his arms, blurred his vision. The birds were everywhere. He was losing his grip; he was going to fall.

He was going to die. He was sure.

On the cliff face, Uncle John lost his footing. He pulled heavily on the rope around Edward's waist; Edward tried to hang on to the wooden spike wedged into the crevice above him but his hand was bloody from the birds' attack, too slippery to get a good hold.

He could hear Uncle John's gruff grunts and his feet scrambling frantically against the rock wall.

Edward tried to get a better hold of the rope above him, but Uncle John was dragging him down.

Edward's father was shouting. "Dammit, John. You're going to kill us all. We're all going to die."

Uncle John was hollering, "Help, me, Edward. Help me, George. Do something."

George reached back to Edward with his knife, "Take my blade, Son. Cut the rope between you and Uncle John. Don't think, just cut it now!"

The noise was shattering his reason; was that Uncle John screaming, the birds shrieking, or his own piercing cries that echoed through the canyon?

Edward hadn't found the intruder in Shelby House. He ran down the stairs slipping and sliding in a mad rush to the backyard where he knelt in the sodden grass and trembled. He should have known better. His father couldn't even get across the threshold. The house, or was it Uncle John, didn't want them inside.

Edward needed to see Esther. He wasn't sure why—maybe just to make sure she was safe, maybe as penance for taking her out of her home against her will. She was at their home now, sleeping deeply. His father had drugged her. As a mortician, George had access to all kinds of drugs.

Edward slipped into the room. Esther was barely breathing, yet alive, so heavily drugged her breath was almost stilled.

He stared at her face in repose and once again saw her as she had looked all those years ago. He remembered seeing that same face as she looked down over the cliff. He knew why his father had her drugged to the brink of death. His father was protecting him, again.

Edward had cut the rope. Edward had killed his uncle and Esther had watched.

As all the dark memories came back, Edward slid to the floor beside Esther's bed.

He was on the cliff face yet again. He was between his Uncle John and his father; Uncle John was pulling heavily on the rope; he was dragging Edward down.

His father was shouting.

Uncle John was hollering.

"Take this knife. Cut the rope, Son. Don't think, just cut it now! He attacked you in your bed. He wanted your blood. It was him!"

A huge dark shape covered Edward, lowered itself on him—threatened to pierce him again. Blood covered his body, tears blurred his vision. The blood was everywhere, he could not wash it off. He was losing his grip—his grip on the rope, his grip on his sanity.

"Take this knife. Don't think, Son. Just cut the rope. John was in your bed that night, he was going to take your blood. Now he's lost his footing; his incompetence will kill us all. Why should we all die? Cut the damn rope! Now."

Esther watched him cut the rope. She watched John plunge to his death. But she wouldn't understand why; why John was no longer worthy of any risk of their part; why he deserved to die. Hell, she wanted eternal life, too. Now that she was finally out of her house she would talk.

George had done so much to protect his son. Edward would do his part, too.

Edward slid the pillow from beneath Esther's head and grasped one end in each hand—but he paused. As he studied Esther's peaceful face her last breath sighed from her lungs without his assistance.

After a moment he put the pillow back under her head and smoothed her hair with a steady hand.

"Hugh had nothing to do with this. Hugh must go home."

Edward looked around the room in panic–he was alone–he must have imagined the voice. He was overtired from the trip, from removing Aunt Esther from her home–so many familial duties, now his guilt about Hugh was driving him to hear voices.

He kissed Aunt Esther's forehead, "I have so many regrets, Aunt Esther," he squeezed her hand gently, "But I promise you–I shall take care of Hugh."

He walked back to Shelby House. His father's carriage was there, in front of the chapel, the rectangular wooden crate still in the back.

He heard cries, they sounded as if they were coming from under the house. He went into the house. He stood still, held his breath, and listened.

Edward stopped at the top step before entering the cellar. Again, he had no light, he hadn't thought to bring one. But he had followed this path so many times. He plunged ahead, following the cries.

He felt his way across the cellar to the butler's lift. He squeezed into the lift, it wasn't as large as he remembered. After removing his gloves, he patted the walls with his hands. He found the panel, slid it to the side, and stepped into the labyrinth.

Again, the walls of the passage were much closer than he remembered. It was disconcerting.

Stay to the left, he remembered, stay to the left. The maze was damp. The ground was mushy. He came to a dead end.

That wasn't right. There were no dead ends.

He felt the walls around him and it seemed there was no way out. He couldn't even find the passage he had followed in.

58

Then he heard the clacking again. The sound of the boy's string and wooden puppet.

"Who's there? Is that you, boy? Hello?" But of course, the boy would have grown up by now. Thoughts raced through his feverish mind, Edward's heart pinched when a small, soft hand slid into his.

Yet he followed the gentle urging of the little hand. As they walked he could hear the Limber Guy's wooden bones jangle together and, as frightful as it would have been if he had let himself think it through, somehow it was comforting to him.

"Hugh had nothing to do with this. Hugh must go home."

That voice again, not a child's voice, and the child was no longer there—his hand was empty now, he cupped around a sudden void.

Edward reached forward and felt the bolts in the chapel door. Quietly he slid the bolts and entered the chapel.

Hugh's pale body lay naked on the altar, candles glowed by his head and feet. Odiferous flowers surrounded him. Edward's father sat on the altar next to Hugh. Edward could see his profile, he was crying. Despite the cold, George was naked too. His body was covered with horrific sores, large and small.

George petted Hugh's cheek lightly as you would a new born kitten, "Youth. Perfection. Beauty. I pray I am not too late to take it for myself."

His hand trembled.

It was the attitude of reverence that gave George away to his son. That and the cries that rose from his pent up soul as he pulled a silver syringe from Hugh's thigh and plunged it into his own.

Edward knew then it hadn't been Uncle John in his bed at all. The enormity of the deception, the betrayal of trust crushed him. In his quest for youth his father had come to his own son's bed. Now Edward remembered the needle clearly– a quick glimpse of the silver syringe in the dim light. He remembered the tiny sores that took so long to heal.

The guilt and shame he had carried over what he thought had gone on in his bed—what of that shame? The burden had been so much a part of him and now suddenly it was gone, replaced by a horror—a madness—a different disgrace.

He couldn't breathe.

He couldn't see.

He lurched back into the labyrinth.

Enough is enough. He would go get the police.

He would tell them everything. He would take his punishment for killing his uncle. But he couldn't face his father.

He stayed to the right this time. He ran and ran. Out of breath he got to the end of the passages, to the door to the butler's lift.

It wouldn't open. He pulled, he strained. He couldn't get out.

"Hugh had nothing to do with this. Hugh must go home."

"Uncle John?" Edward recognized the voice now.

Then Edward heard Esther's voice, "What is this? Where am I? Am I home?"

"Yes, my dear, you're home now." Uncle John replied tenderly.

"What's happened to me? As I walked through the yards, gardens I had thought so magnificent were but mud and weeds, wild grasses grew where I had seen the gardenias and the rose bushes. The flowers for my vases, arrangements – who had placed them so carefully every morning?" Particles of light gathered in the dark until a much younger Aunt Esther stood in the passage beside him.

"It was me, Esther." Uncle John approached from Edward's left, carrying Esther's sable cloak over his arm, "George ripped me away from you too soon."

"John, Shelby House was heaven. I wish I had known the wonders came from you."

"I had no voice, Esther." Edward lowered his eyes respectfully as Uncle John wrapped the cloak around her and pulled her into his arms.

"Why do you now? Why do I?"

"You are newly dead. And I am now horrible in my wrath. I am strong because I have vengeance to wield. Hugh must come home to Shelby House unharmed. Edward will help."

"Edward? Oh, my little Ned?" Esther said, "Where is he?"

"I'm here, Aunt Esther." Edward was shaking. "I'm going to turn myself in. I'm going to tell them, Uncle John. I'll take what's coming to me."

"No, Ned. No. It wasn't your fault. I absolve you. You were deceived into madness. You can still find redemption for your little sins. Go get Hugh and bring him back to Shelby House. I'll deal with my cursed brother. Now hurry, hurry. Rescue Hugh. He is an innocent."

Edward's heart broke as he listened.

"But Uncle John–" Edward closed his eyes. "Hugh hung himself the day he found me with Lilly."

"I know. Bring Hugh to us, bring him home to Shelby House. I've only let your father live to keep Shelby House in the family for Esther. But I think you can take over now." His voice hardened, "George has definitely come to the end of his rope."

Edward was resolved, he would bring Hugh home.

In the cold stone chapel a massive hand thrust thick fingers through George Shelby's chest, shattered bone, gripped his cold heart, and began to twist.

Edward walked into the chapel and approached the altar where Hugh lay.

Edward looked at Hugh's beauty with massive confusion in his heart, the salt air blew in the door, and Hugh opened his eyes, "Ned! You've come for me. Come back with me to Shelby House. Do you remember, we were children here? Do you remember the labyrinth?" He sat up on the altar, tears in his eyes, his lower lip trembled, "Oh, Ned! I want us to stay here forever."

Edward pulled Hugh into his arms, "Yes. We will live here in Shelby House together for all of my days...and beyond."

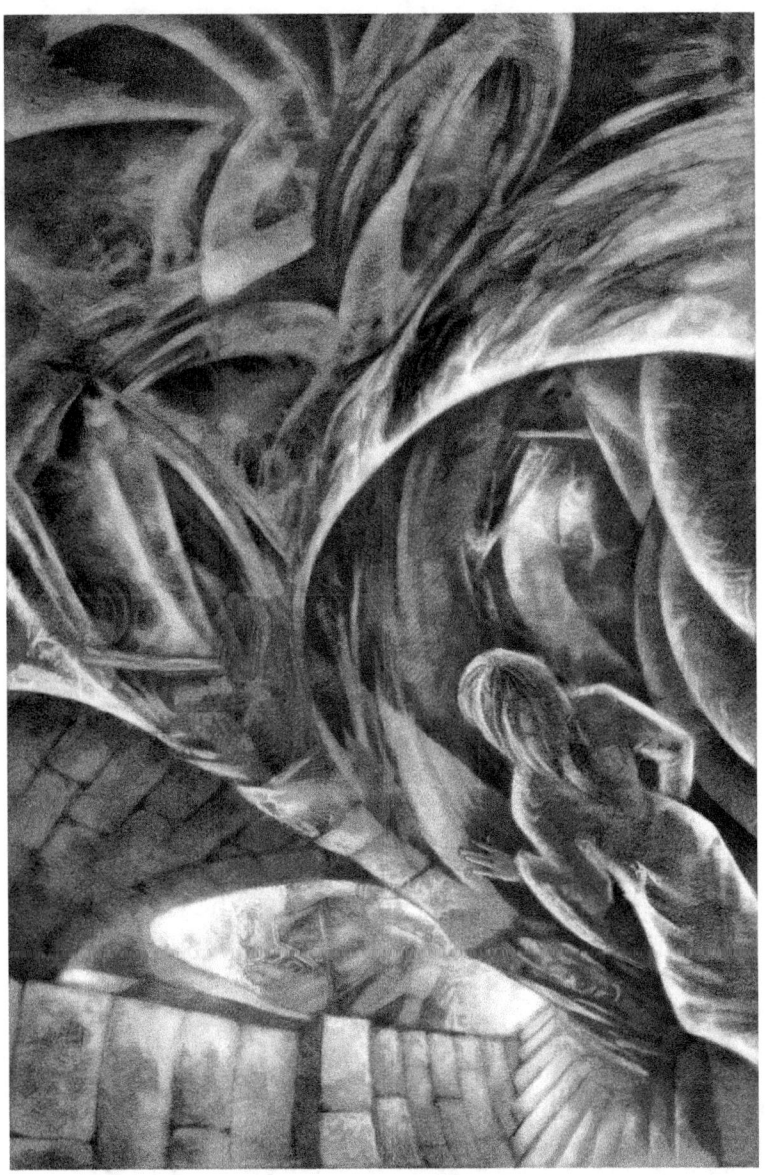

Illustration by P. Emerson Williams

Hollenstein

by DJ Tyrer

I smoothed the lap of my dress, feeling incredibly self-conscious as I rode in the carriage toward Castle Hollenstein. Toward Otto. Toward a new beginning for my life.

Having been rejected by my family, my thoughts naturally turned to Otto's offer of sanctuary. I had been banned from contact with him, but had ignored the prohibition. Now, it seemed he was the only one to whom I could turn. I just had to hope his love would prove constant, unlike that of my parents, who feared social ostracism for my 'antics', as they termed my decision.

I turned and leaned my head out the window to view the Bavarian countryside and marvel at its mountains. Home for me was – had been – a townhouse in Brussels, as unlike this region as could be. In a sense, it seemed suitable: my future would be as unlike my past as it could be.

What had been beautiful country grew gloomy. As the carriage left the paved highway for the rutted track that would lead us to the castle, the countryside began to change. The verdant Bavarian hillsides were replaced by a woodland of horribly twisted and stunted trees. Even the ground, carpeted with pine needles, had an unpleasant greyness to it, so that the entire area appeared as if it were subject to some blight.

The scene did nothing to dispel my nerves nor to raise my spirits. Even the sunlight seemed to fade, despite the sickly trees not rising high enough to block its rays. I shivered. It felt colder, too, unless that was an illusion from the unwholesome atmosphere of the district.

The track grew steeper and the carriage slowed, the horses finding it more and more difficult to pull it up the slope. Here the woods gave way to grey-looking gorse that clung tenaciously to the steep mountainside, despite seeming frail and diseased.

The castle sat atop the mountain, a low, squat edifice designed for defence rather than beauty. Why it was placed there, I had no idea. Yes, it was a defensible position, but it overlooked nothing but the unpromising woods below and a black, lonely tarn. There were no settlements for it to ward, nor a significant route for it to watch over, nor border to guard. Perhaps there had been something when it was built three centuries ago, but today it was more like the abandoned ruins that were lair to some horror in a mediocre gothic novel, lacking reason for it to be as it is.

I didn't much like the look of the place. It was intended as a fortress not a home and looked cold and uncomfortable. I tried to recall if Otto had said whether it was possessed of modern conveniences. I remembered he had mentioned installing electric lighting, but that seemed far too modern for such a history-laden building as this. Still, I hoped my memory was correct. I should prefer the steady glow of a wire filament to the wan flicker of a candle in the shadowed passages within its thick stone walls.

Not that I could blame Otto for either its aspect or its seeming state of disrepair. He had inherited it a few years earlier from an uncle, who had spent most of his time in Munich. Otto, in his turn, had largely avoided it until recently. Still, I was grateful for the offer of sanctuary, no matter its appearance.

I shivered again as we drew near it. The castle had a chill, exposed aspect, but more than that there was a vastness to it. Although from a distance it had appeared squat, and it was when compared to other castles with their soaring watchtowers, up close it towered high above the carriage, while its sheer bulk was awesome. Going through its wide, deep gate arch was rather too much like passing below beneath the overhang of a cliff and I retracted my head within the carriage, lest it collapse upon us. Not that the coach body could resist such an onslaught. I told myself such thoughts were irrational, but given its age, who could say whether the archway yet retained its integrity?

Clattering its way across the cobbled courtyard, the carriage came to a halt before the steps leading to the door of the castle keep. Rather than the grand marble sweep of stairs up to the glass doors of some fairytale chateau, these steps were utilitarian and narrow, running up the keep wall to a small, ironbound door of oak.

Standing at the bottom of the steps, waiting to receive me, were three figures. Otto, of course, and his manservant, Piet. The third was a girl, slightly younger than me, who I assumed was the maidservant he said he would engage for my arrival. There was also a cook and housekeeper, I knew, but of her there was no sign.

Otto stepped up to the carriage door and opened it for me. He held out his hand and I gratefully took it to steady myself. Otto was more than twenty years older than me, tall and lithe. His carefully-shaped beard emphasised the aristocratic features I found so attractive.

"Greetings, Johanna," he said, leaning in to kiss my cheek.

"It's good to see you," I replied, hugging him.

As we stepped apart and Otto offered me his elbow, the coachman tossed my baggage down to Piet. Otto's man had declined since last I had seen him in Brussels, with two or three days' worth of stubble and the stink of stale beer about him. As he hefted my trunk, he tottered and I wondered if he were half-drunk.

His job done, the coachman returned to his seat, turned the carriage and set off, keen to be away.

"Johanna, this is Lisel," said Otto, nodding at the girl. "Lisel will be your lady's maid."

"Hello, Lisel," I said with a smile. "It is very nice to meet you."

She stuttered a reply and curtsied awkwardly.

"No need to be shy," I told her, then Otto was leading me up the stairs and into the keep, Lisel trailing after us.

"Piet is taking your things up to your suite. I had him and Frau Gruber prepare it for you and make sure it was clean. This place became quite a mess these past decades; I do not believe it is a place that could ever be loved."

"Will we live here when...?" I wanted to finish that sentence, but the barriers seemed insurmountable.

"When you are my wife?" he said, kissing the top of my head. "Oh, no. Then, we shall have a townhouse in Munich, or wherever you wish."

"But..."

"Do not concern yourself, my dear. You shall be my bride. I have it all planned."

"Then, you will be able to... cure me?"

He nodded and kissed my head again. "Yes. It's all ready. Relax for a few days, then you'll be ready."

That was how I had met Otto, how our love had begun. He was a doctor, although, thanks to his inheritance, he did not need to practice professionally. He took on the occasional commission from those of his social circle and their friends and families. Specialising in both mental and physical disorders, my parents had asked him to examine me. As soon as he heard the details of my case he had eagerly done so, but when it became clear his proposed cure was not the one my parents desired, his services had been dispensed with. Despite that, and to my parents' intense annoyance, we continued to see one another socially until my parents sought to confine me to my room.

Regardless of my parents' feelings and the whispers of the moral arbiters behind their fans, Otto had never been ashamed of me. Of course, after the first giddy wave of love and liberation, I had begun to worry if his interest were solely professional, or even prurient, but his desire was real and he always had maintained he would marry me, and now it seemed that truly would take place.

"Lisel will show you the rest of the way," he said, detaching his arm from mine. "I have work to do. I will see you at supper." He kissed my hand, smiled and walked away.

I glanced at the girl who appeared disconcerted.

"Uh, this way, my, uh, my lady," she said, curtseying before setting off down the corridor. She lapsed into silence until we arrived at my suite, then asked, "Is it true?"

"Is what true?" I asked, attempting to keep my tone even. Such questions inevitably preceded unpleasantness in my experience.

"Is it true that you're a... you're a boy?"

"No," I spat, crossly.

"But, Doctor Hessler said..." Lisel started, quailing a little.

"I am an urning," I told her, coldly. "We are... a third sex, Ulrichs says. I was born with the... physical characteristics of a male, but I am female, I assure you. My body is... misaligned, I suppose is the word. Otto – Doctor Hessler – has been studying the way to cure me, realign me."

"Make you into a woman?" Lisel prompted.

"Yes," I finished, simply.

"So, it's medical?"

"Yes." That answer seemed to reassure her and she went about opening my trunk and cases so that I could choose an outfit for supper.

Despite her apparent relief, she continued to seem nervous and ill-at-ease as I washed.

"Lisel, am I really that terrible?" I had to ask. "Do I upset you so much?"

"Oh, no, my lady," she gasped, helping me dry myself. "It's not you. Well, not much," she admitted with a blush. "Although you will take a little getting used to, I admit. No, it's this place."

"The castle?" I picked out a yellow gown and she began to help me dress.

She nodded.

"Why? I mean, yes it is a little messy, a little spooky, but..."

"No, it's not that. It's the curse."

"The curse?"

"No, the Hollenstein itself. They say it's the capstone to Hell. The witches used to hold their sabbat here on Walpurgisnacht and the castle remains full of evil. I should never have come, but my mother is dead and, well, life is hard for a girl with no prospects and, the doctor, he was offering such a good wage, even if you did sound odd, if you'll excuse me for saying so."

"Indeed, I do," I said, pleased she cared about offending me.

"But, was it worth it?" Lisel finished. "I don't know."

"Well, is there actually anything to worry you?"

She shook her head as she finished linking the hooks of my dress. "No, not really. It's spooky and there are sometimes odd sounds and lights from the dungeon where the doctor has been working; I'm not sure on what," she added, forestalling my question. I wondered if it was something to do with me.

Dressed, I descended to the dining hall, where Lisel departed to eat her meal in the kitchen.

It was only Otto and I at the table, creating an enjoyable intimacy, and Frau Gruber attended only long enough to serve us before heading off to dine with Piet and Lisel. It was clear she disapproved of me, but basking in Otto's love, I didn't care. I was happy. At last, I would have my happy ending.

Lisel was right about sounds from the dungeon. Up in my suite, we could hear the noise of something throbbing below us, echoing up gloomy stairwells and along shadowed corridors.

"You hear, miss?" Lisel said.

"It sounds like a machine," I replied. But, the thought was not so comforting. An engine might not be a devil, but it was strange and unnatural.

"I'm going to take a look," I told her the third night we heard the sounds. Otto had deflected my attempts to ask him about what he was doing when we were together and, at those times, it didn't seem so important. Unlike now when the darkness made it seem all the more ominous.

"You wait here," I said, pulling a shawl over my shoulders. She had made as if to accompany me, but it was clear she was not steeled to do so and I slipped from my bedroom, candle in hand. The electric lighting Otto had installed was in only a few key rooms and was prone to unreliability, flickering and dimming erratically.

My skirts swished on the stairs as I descended toward the dungeon. The flicker of the candle flame cast skittering shadows across the stairwell's walls. Below me, a weak bluish glow flickered. Had I not known Otto was down there at work, I could easily have imagined Lisel's gateway to Hell had been opened and its imps released.

Arriving at the bottom of the stairs, I paused to wipe a cobweb from my face and hair and to discern in which direction I should proceed. The thrum was much stronger here, seeming almost to vibrate the flagstones beneath my feet and surround me. When the bluish flash came again, I saw it was to my left, so I followed the passage in that direction.

Although I doubted the dungeons had been used for their original purpose in centuries, they retained their heavy, ironbound doors. It was from behind one of these that the glow emanated. I tried it. It was locked.

I knocked. "Otto, it's me, Johanna." I had to shout due to the noise. My hair was up on end; there was electricity in the air.

I banged on the door again and called his name.

The door opened a crack. I jumped at the sudden movement. Otto looked at me through the gap, almost a silhouette against the blue light, which shadowed his features in a ghastly fashion. I shuddered involuntarily and the movement of his lips

71

failed to reassure me, seeming more like a horrible than a welcoming smile.

"Oh, Johanna, it's you – what do you want?"

"What's happening?"

"I'm working."

"At what?" I pressed.

"I'm preparing your cure. One last test of the equipment to ensure it is correctly calibrated."

"Oh, I thought it was going to be an operation. What is the electricity for?"

Despite my desire to become the woman I was supposed to be, I had always been nervous about the idea of having an operation. Otto had promised me it would be fine. I wondered if the electricity was something to do with the anaesthetic. I remembered Otto telling me electricity could affect the muscles and the brain. Perhaps this was some new procedure he was perfecting.

"Nothing to worry about," he assured me with another ghastly, shadowed smile. "Just something to ensure everything goes as desired. Shall we go ahead tomorrow?"

Perhaps it was being asked there in the horrible glow that made me feel so nervous. As much as I wanted it, it was an enormous step to take. To have the question posed by that ghoulish, leering face was hardly reassuring.

Still... I nodded. "Yes, tomorrow."

"Go to bed. Get some sleep."

I nodded and walked away, hoping my dreams would not be filled with nightmares of Otto's twisted visage and thoughts of some diabolical machinery in a cobwebbed dungeon. I was to be disappointed. I awoke drenched in sweat and called for Lisel, but there was no response.

I rose and washed and dressed myself, trying to banish nightmarish thoughts from my mind. I looked down at myself and as I did so realised this would be my last day trapped in this body. I decided to stick to my shift and dressing gown for ease of undressing for the operation. A while later, there was a knock at my door and Frau Gruber entered with breakfast on a tray, a task Lisel normally carried out.

I asked the housekeeper where Lisel was, wondering if she was ill.

"Day off," she replied. She still seemed to barely tolerate my existence.

"I didn't realise she had a day off. She said nothing."

She shrugged. "Master says you will go down to him at ten. He says you know where to go."

I nodded. "I do."

She said nothing else, but turned and walked away.

I sat and picked at the schnitzel, unable to summon much of an appetite, nerves nagging at me. I was a bit nonplussed at Lisel's absence. I had been looking forward to having her around as a source of moral support, but reasoned Otto had given her the day off as I would doubtless be unconscious for much of it. Probably, she would be there when I awoke, to help look after me. Yet, it didn't quite seem right. Where had she gone? The trip to the nearest settlement would devour much of the day, rendering the trip a waste of time, as far as I could see. Would she be away for days? I hoped not. I needed her. If nothing else, unlike Frau Gruber, she was a friendly face. Indeed, the more I considered her absence, the less happy with it I became, even if my concerns were nebulous.

Not that I had long to worry about it, for the clock soon chimed quarter to ten and I realised it was nearly time for me to join Otto in the dungeon. I didn't want to keep him – or myself – waiting. I headed downstairs.

Despite it being mid-morning, below the castle it may as well have been midnight. The machine wasn't running, so there wasn't even its intermittent glow to light my way, the wan candlelight sending nervous shadows slipping along the passage walls.

I reached the door to the chamber where Otto had been last night. I raised my hand to knock, then paused. I don't know why, but I decided instead to ease the door open and step inside without announcing my presence. Unlike the night before, it was unlocked.

Inside, I no longer required my candle and snuffed its flame, for the chamber had been provided with electric light. The doorway was at the top of a short staircase that ran parallel to the wall, descending to floor level. The high vaulted ceiling reminded me of a church and, with a shock, I realised that, amongst the cables, tables of equipment and scientific instruments, sat the Hollenstein itself, the capstone of Hell of which Lisel had spoken. I had always liked to tell myself that stories of ghosts and witches were mere superstition, nothing more than nonsense, but now I had to wonder if this were the gathering place of witches for celebrations of their sabbat on Walpurgisnacht. Was this a church to the Devil? What had possessed – and I instantly regretted thinking in those terms – Otto to make use of this particular chamber?

For a moment, I tried to rationalise his decision, thinking that, perhaps, it was for convenience, because of its size, for there was a large machine at the far end of the dungeon that, I guessed, probably generated the electricity. But, then, I saw that spikes of iron had been hammered into the stone and cables run from them. I tried to tell myself there was some logical, scientific explanation, but my thoughts kept returning to what Lisel had said about it being the capstone... Just what was going on? I didn't like it.

Otto and his manservant, Piet, were in the chamber below me.

"Nearly ten," Otto said. "Time to increase the power."

Piet nodded and took a swig from the bottle he was holding.

"Must you?" Otto snapped at him. "I need you sober, this is delicate work."

"Little strumpet clawed me," he slurred back.

"Well, she's out now," Otto replied, nodding toward a table covered by a white cloth. With a start, I realised there was the swell of a body beneath the shroud.

"Who is that?" I demanded, trying to keep my voice from quavering. "Who is under that sheet?"

They both turned to look up at me in surprise.

"Ah, Johanna," Otto began in his best doctorly voice, "you're here. A little early, but eager to proceed, eh?"

"I asked you a question," I snapped. "Who is that? What are you doing?"

"What am I doing? Well, my dear, I'm about to cure you of your unfortunate condition. As to who that is," he stepped over to the table and pulled back the sheet, "I'm sure you recognise your maid."

It was Lisel. "I don't understand."

"The Hollenstein has some amazing properties," he said. "As you know, the mind is an

75

electrical process within the brain. Well, the stone has some chemical in its makeup that facilitates the transfer of mental energies between two bodies. I will attach her and you to it with these cables and, with the appropriate charge, shall cause your minds to migrate and swap places."

I stared at him in shock.

Perhaps he took my stunned silence for approval, for he seemed to preen slightly, as he concluded, "You shall be what you always wanted to be and I shall be able to marry you – and all without some risky, physical operation."

I must admit I was tempted. But, then, I thought of Lisel lying there, drugged and helpless. "What happens to her? When she's in my body, I mean."

"We cannot let her live, I'm afraid. She would be a liability. It is a shame, I know, but she is only a servant."

"I cannot believe you are so callous," I gasped.

"Pragmatic, my dear," he replied with a smile that recalled to my mind the ghoulish leer of the night before.

"You chose the right place," I spat, "this Devil's church: you're a devil, Otto – a devil!"

"You are overwrought. Come and let us begin."

"I shall not! You want to murder Lisel – me – I - It's wrong!"

"But, you want to be a woman, don't you?"

"Not at her expense! And not at the loss of my body. I want to be reshaped, not become someone else."

"You'll still be you. You'll still be the same mind."

"But, I'm not just a mind. All of this is me, for better and for worse. I want to change, not become someone else entirely."

"Well, my dear, that just will not do. Now, I know best: do as I say." He turned and twisted a knob on the generator.

"No!" I declared. "No," I repeated, more softly. "I won't."

Otto swore. "Bring her down," he told Piet as casually as requesting a book from a high shelf.

His manservant swayed his way across the chamber to the stairs. I looked around for something with which to defend myself. There was an ancient, rusted sconce on the wall, left over from before Otto brought his vile electricity into that dungeon. I seized it, tugged and pulled it easily from the wall in a shower of rust fragments.

"Stay back!" I cried, but he didn't seem to hear me.

Piet started to climb the stairs. I swung the sconce and smashed it into the side of his head. He looked at me stupidly, blinked once, then fell backwards down the stairs, sprawling unconscious at the bottom.

Otto didn't seem to have noticed, busied by his infernal machinery.

"Put her on the table," he called without looking around.

His disdainful tone stoked the anger within me into a raging fire. The way he was treating me as his property, to be disposed of as he wished, regardless of my wishes, and his complete disregard for Lisel, who had been so sweet, so kind to me. It brought bile to my throat, disgusted me.

I was hardly thinking as I descended the stairs and crossed the dungeon to where he stood. The fiend

– I no longer felt any love for him – remained oblivious to my presence. I would kill him, and Lisel and I would flee and start a new life. She could help me pass as a woman. There was probably money or valuables we could take to fund a fresh start. He was completely unaware as I raised the sconce once more before bringing it down into the back of his head.

The blow smashed him face forward into the machine, his hand skewing the dial. It exploded in a shower of sparks and spitting flames. There was a terrible sound mixed with his screams and a blinding glow. Then, the chamber fell silent and was plunged into darkness, save for the light of the flames that licked about Otto's slumped corpse.

There was a sudden shriek behind me and I jumped. Turning, I saw Lisel sitting up. She tried to stand, but sprawled onto the floor, the anaesthetic clearly still affecting her. The sudden surge of electricity down the cables attached to her brow had clearly shocked her awake.

I ran to help her.

"Lisel! Lisel, are you alright?"

She turned her head and spat, "You tried to kill me!"

"Lisel, it's me, Johanna. Otto's dead. You're safe."

"You killed me!" she shrieked, grabbing for a scalpel from a nearby table and trying to slash me. It was then that the subtle change in her voice struck me and I realised what had happened.

"You've killed my body," she sobbed, "and trapped me in the same hell as you."

I stared in shock and didn't even react when she – he – attempted again to slash me. I was lucky the anaesthetic, which Otto had used on Lisel, was still in effect despite the jolt of energy, or I would have been dead.

Feeling an enormous guilt, I stepped back and looked down at Lisel's body, in which the mind of Otto was now trapped. It was bad enough to have attempted to kill him, but to find I had killed Lisel with that same action...

"I'll kill you..." she mumbled.

I picked up a heavy piece of equipment, neither knowing nor caring what its original purpose was, and took a step forward.

"I'm sorry," I murmured, whether to Otto or Lisel or both of them, I wasn't sure, then raised the item and brought it down with a scream.

I felt disgusted with myself, as I never had before. Murder had not been my intention. Indeed, the course of events had been thrust upon me by Otto's madness. Yet, I was unable to shake the thought that I had acted of my own free will; that their blood was on my hands.

The authorities would doubtless apportion blame solely upon me. I already knew their opinion of my sort. They said we were mad. They would think this another manifestation of my lunacy. They would never believe me.

To think that minutes before I had thought my troubles at an end, my dreams come true. Now, I was trapped in a nightmare and all hope had been lost.

There was only one course left to me, now. Quickly, I ascended from the dungeon and climbed one of the squat castle's square towers. Below me a cliff fell away. I gazed down into the abyss and prepared to embrace it.

Leave

by Stephanie Ellis

The first guests had started to arrive. I could hear them downstairs, muffled laughter, the swish of silks, the clink of glasses. When I was small I loved to watch the carriages taking elegant ladies and their beaus to the theatre, dreaming that one day I would be amongst them.

Now, in a way, that dream has come true but I am on the other side, the performer, the entertainer. When Gregory first found me, he would tell of the stages on which he performed, the audiences he commanded, the lords and ladies, the princes. He promised me that world of colour. And I believed him. I always believed him, even when his eyes betrayed his words.

Gregory does not allow me to mix with the company. He says they will contaminate my thoughts and that I need to keep my mind clear – pure – so here I am, locked away in my little room to which only he has the key. The servants do not speak to me. I see their looks and know what they think of me, what they think I am to him. He does nothing to disabuse them of this notion. He finds it amusing that they think a man such as he would ever share my bed. I am fallen and he is my saviour. Yet another lie.

I'm never quite sure what happens to me at these gatherings. I know Gregory has supreme control over my will; I could no more resist him than a moth the flame. I can only remember the chain, its delicate silver links shimmering in front of me, swinging back and forth, taking my eyes, my thoughts ... and myself.

The murmuring below has grown louder. There are more people here now. Soon I will be released from my cell. I strain my ears. Snatched conversations float up.

"... I heard she cured Lord Eastley's son."

"... It was amazing, almost as if she had become the boy herself."

"... Mr. Faradon is truly the greatest hypnotist of our times."

"... but don't you think such manipulation of another's mind is dangerous ..."

I have lost count of the number of performances I have given. All I know is that after every event I am left exhausted and with an ailment or complaint from which I had not previously suffered. I remember that boy, Lord Eastley's son. I remember speaking to him in the dark, discovering the creeping sickness within, tasting the poison that had spread through his body. I was able to tell his family the cause of his suffering. The doctors had been sceptical but they had examined him in the light of my findings and saw that I spoke the truth. The gratitude of Lord Eastley allowed Gregory to buy this house.

Occasionally I have overheard descriptions of my performance; I will wince and scowl, cough and shake. Sometimes I frighten these watchers with a fit, foaming from the mouth like a rabid dog. But their fascination outweighs their horror and keeps them glued to their seats waiting for my final dénouement. From what people say it is as if the illness that affected the patient has transferred itself to me. Gregory says I am not really ill, that it's all in the mind. Yet each time it takes me a little longer to recover.

I hear footsteps, slow, heavy outside my door. He is coming to prepare me. I wish I could say no. I have tried so hard to fight him off, keep his voice out of my head but I am too weak, too feeble.

He is here now, standing at the foot of my bed, that mocking, superior smile on his face. He always stands there, silently regarding me before he tells me what is to happen in a performance. I am not his assistant, I am his possession, his puppet. My parents gave me to him. I would be one less mouth to feed. Poverty meant they did not question his motives. Gregory was, after all, a gentleman – wasn't he?

"Ah, Alice," he sighs. There is a gleam of satisfaction in his eyes. "I trust you are refreshed?"

I give my usual answer. I nod.

He is holding his right hand close to my face. I can see that delicate chain wrapped around his fingers, a small cross hangs from it. The crucifixion. Tonight and every night I feel it is I who am crucified, the sacrificial lamb to his growing ego. He swings the chain slowly back and forth. I nod mutely. I can give no other answer, already I am sinking, disappearing from myself. Soon I too will become part of the audience leaving only a tiny remnant of me watching on, helpless.

"We have good company tonight Alice, truly deserving of something amazing." He rubs his hands in anticipation. "Tonight we have been graced with the presence of a prince of Spain no less! Did I not promise you that one day you would perform in front of royalty?"

No wonder he looks so happy, so full of pride. Gregory has put on his finest suit, cut to perfection. It gives him a distinguished air. Respectable, scientific, almost aristocratic, he has erased all traces of the gutter from which he came, from which I came. I doubt he even uses his real name. We have both been reinvented.

Again I nod. He takes my unresisting hand and raises me up. I stare into those dark, dark eyes of his but I cannot read what they hide. His words force me to smile, to share in his triumph.

"Tonight I have planned a treat for them," he continued. "I will show them the true power of the mesmerist, my power, in all its glory. After tonight I will be feted in the greatest houses in the land. My fortune will be made." A self-satisfied smile plays on the corner of his mouth. A sharp contrast to the cruelty he usually exhibits.

He makes no mention of my part in this, the contribution I will make to his performance, the vital part I play. He does not share the takings with me although he has bought me a new dress for tonight.

He speaks. "I need absolute obedience tonight, Alice."

I don't know why he is saying that. I always obey, I have no choice. I nod.

"I have made discreet enquiries about our patient. The boy is Sir Meecham's only son and heir. A weakly fellow, nobody has ever been able to say quite what's wrong with him. Even the best doctors of Harley Street have drawn a blank but tonight I will cure him. I will become as a God." His eyes bore into me, forcing my acquiescence, my complicity.

I nod.

He is still moving the cross back and forth, back and forth, in front of me.

"We will start in the usual way," he says. "I will give the command and you will enter his mind, describe how you feel – how he feels, what he senses."

I nod. Why he is telling me this I do not know. It is what I always have to do. Even so I commit his words to memory. If I get something wrong I will suffer.

83

He stops swinging the chain and lowers his face to mine. I wish I could turn away, his eyes burn me with their intensity. He is looking for something but whatever answer I have mutely given is obviously the right one.

"Then I will command you to enter him completely," he continues. "I will command your soul to leave your body and take possession of the boy's."

I freeze. This is wrong. He has never ordered me to do this. My blood has turned to ice, sheer terror has taken hold. Run, run, a small part of me is screaming. But I can't run, he is in my head, he controls me. My feet stay solidly in place and all I can do is nod.

He leads me along the corridor. My hand on his arm. One of the maids sees me and smirks. Then she notices my dress and I see the envy in her eyes. Perhaps she is wondering what she needs to do to get a dress such as mine. Gregory ignores her. She is invisible to him. And she knows it.

I am looking down into a hall ablaze with light and laughter. The world I wanted to be part of is there before me but all I see are the shadows that dance at the edges and I know I have been condemned to stand forever on the outside looking in.

Now he is guiding me down the stairs. The fine lords and ladies gaze curiously up at me as I descend. Some look a little disappointed. I am no great beauty, no waif or stray to excite any pity. I let them down with my plainness. I am easily forgettable, I have to be, it is Gregory who holds centre stage. I wonder briefly who the royal patron is but the lamps are dimmed and faces fall into shadow. They all look the same.

I take my seat as the audience gathers in a semi-circle around me. Gregory is shaking hands and exchanging pleasantries with his admirers. He is in his element, this is his court. He no longer bows to those who come to see him. He considers himself their equal. I wonder if they feel the same about him.

Another seat stands empty by my side. This is for the boy we are supposed to cure. Silence falls as he enters the room. His father leads him forward, a gawky lad, pale and graceless, a poor specimen indeed. We are a well-matched pair.

He is looking at me enquiringly, no doubt wondering what sort of creature I am. There is nothing I can do or say. I am not permitted.

"Your Royal Highness, my lords, ladies and gentlemen," Gregory has begun, hands raised, a conductor guiding his orchestra. He relishes this role. "Prepare yourselves for a true marvel. Never before has such a feat been seen in our great city or anywhere else in the world. Only here will you witness true psychic ability. Watch and wonder."

I see a few smirk at his words but Gregory does not notice. His pride drives him tonight.

While he talks the chain has started to swing innocently back and forth in his hand. My eyes are drawn to it and the audience begins to fade but not before I take a final look at the boy's face, noting that it bears a cynical and rather superior expression. Gregory continues.

"Many dispute the nature of the soul, whether it can exist as a separate entity free from the constraints of the body, whether it can infiltrate the flesh of another. Indeed is it for God only to command this ethereal aspect of our lives?"

There is an audible gasp at these words; he is treading dangerous ground.

"Tonight, for the first time ever, you will see the soul of one person enter the body of another." He pauses dramatically. "Tonight, the soul of my young protégé Alice will depart her body at my command and enter that of our patient."

I have not faded so far away that I miss the boy's startled look, his disbelief easily read. I wish I could tell him how lucky he is, how safe. I sense I don't have long left. There are more stirrings amongst the company. I can imagine their excited faces leaning forward, eyes fixed on me as my time comes, as the limelight fixes itself on me.

"Yes, it is hard to believe," says my puppet master surveying the audience with a look that settles them immediately, as if they too are under his spell. "But I will demonstrate both the truth of my claim and cure the boy in front of your very eyes. Watch and prepare to be amazed."

He inclines his head and then turns away from them ... and toward me. He holds the chain close to my face. Back and forth, back and forth. My crucifixion has begun.

"Alice."

The command forces me to look at Gregory. I hate him, I fear him, and all I can do is obey.

"Break those chains that hold you, Alice."

Back and forth.

"Throw off those binds, loosen yourself from your fleshly anchor."

Back and forth.

"I command you, Alice. You must free your mind from the confines of your body, let it drift outside yourself." This has been his mantra at the start of every performance, every hypnosis. Silver glints back and forth.

I nod.

My disappearance begins. I start to feel dizzy. I see darkness and shadow snaking their way towards me, pulling me up and out. Part of me has gone already. I feel empty, bereft. Just a little piece remains, bearing witness, trying to fight back. Silver dances.

"Alice. Tell us what is wrong with this boy."

I cannot resist. I see what the young man sees, feel what he feels. Whether it is real or not, is another matter. I am merely obeying my master. I know the script. Silver burns as it spins.

"Please sir," the voice that comes from me is not mine, it is the voice of a youth, broken, unsure. "I feel as if I'm drowning, there is something flooding my lungs ..."

A doctor's mutterings interrupt me.

"Bah, we've already tested him for tuberculosis. One of the first things we did. The man's a charlatan." The doctor's companions mutter in agreement.

A flicker of annoyance passes over Gregory's face but he swiftly masters himself, keeps his countenance smooth, unruffled. He will make them believe. They will believe.

Silver glances at me.

"Alice. Can you see further?"

I nod.

"Only a little, there are too many shadows to make out anything clearly." It is dark, the dark has always frightened me. Does the audience hear the fear in my voice, can they not see my terror?

"Then you must search beyond these shades."

Somewhere I hear the clock strike the hour. I think my heart has stopped. Something is pressing down on me, squeezing out my last breath. I am so scared. I wish someone would help me. I look around but can see nothing. I am blind. The voice I dread speaks again.

"Alice. You know what you must do." The words batter at me, breaking my will. Please, please. The chain swings.

The Son cast in silver summons me. He cried out for his Father and was abandoned. I have no voice but I too, have been abandoned.

I sit still, a stone statue. I am trying so hard to resist. My master repeats his command. He has never had to repeat himself and I hear the displeasure in his voice. The chain swings closer to me. I imagine blood dripping from the body on the cross. So much blood. Will I bleed in the same way?

Back and forth, back and forth. Now I am further away. Such a deep darkness. I am teetering on the edge of the void.

Silver again. Always silver binding me to my prison, preventing my escape. It is so pretty. See how it dances. I weaken, watch closer. Feel the start of my death.

"Alice!"

This time I nod. I am too tired to fight. The trance has become a heavy blanket suffocating the life out of me. I am too weak to throw it off. The cross continues to swing, I continue to die.

"On my next command, Alice, your soul will leave your body completely and enter into that of the patient."

There is a small gasp from the audience, I can sense Gregory's pride growing; he will not stop now.

Back and forth. Silver is the only light.

It is coming. Please God help me. The cross, the cross ... the body on the cross. It is me. I bear the stigmata. Back and forth. I nod.

The ground falls away from me, crumbling as I crumble. I see nothing, feel nothing to grasp. Please, I whisper into the darkness.

"Alice," Gregory's voice is tense, urgent, all-powerful. "Leave your body, fly."

I am trying not to let go. I can only just cling on to myself. Somewhere I am crying. The chain still swinging, back and forth, back and forth.

"Alice! I order you."

Back and forth.

"Leave your body, leave your earthly shell!"

Back and forth.

Please, please. I am trying but I am slipping away.

There is fury underneath his command. The chain again. Back and forth, back and forth. Binds me with its fetters, shackles me to him. Through the fog his voice is coming, closer, closer. Wrapping itself around my soul, taking possession, pulling me, forcing me out.

"Alice – LEAVE!"

The silver Son dazzles me in its intensity. Those eyes gaze at me with such pity, knowing my pain and terror. They hold out a promise I have never heard spoken before. They speak words of comfort, they are not Gregory's words.

The links are breaking even as they swing before me. Splintering into myriad slivers that pierce the last remnants of my hold on the world I know.

Gregory murmurs something in my ear. I cannot make out what he says but I can almost taste his anger as it roils through the void. I am failing him.

Death swings on the chain. Back and forth.

Silver stars glitter a trail towards me. It is the path I must take. It is my only escape.

I nod and let the darkness claim me.

Illustration by Joshua L. Hood

Speech to the Prometheus League

by Flo Stanton


SPECIAL TO THE TIMES
A Speech to the Prometheus League
A Father's Plea


JULY 14, 1860--Last night at Egyptian Hall followers of the science of burial cremation heard a lecture by the esteemed Mr. Lawrence Upton, former phlebotomist to Her Majesty. If attendees were expecting a medical disquisition propounding the public health benefits of cremation, or a sermon arguing the Biblical justification for it, they did not receive it from Mr. Upton. Allowing the previous speaker to detail the clinical aspects of the subject featured elsewhere in this newspaper, Mr. Upton held his audience spellbound with his personal history, elements of which border the horrific and phantastic, for the better part of an hour, eschewing consultation of any written drafts withal:


"Good evening, ladies and gentlemen. I leave to my associates any discussion of the technical details of this science. I speak to you only as a bereaved father. My story begins—and ends—with my son.

"Edward was a motherless child, my wife having died of puerperal fever. I declined to remarry, both resigning myself to losing the love of my life and vowing not to endanger the life of another fine woman via parturition. I applied myself assiduously to the duties of a parent and may be forgiven for adjudging my son's childhood a contented one, notwithstanding the absence of his mother. To our good fortune my brother lived nearby, and his wife assumed that happy role, herself the mother of twin girls.

"Edward displayed an early artistic aptitude, drawing by age ten faithful representations of animals and people, taking principally pets and members of his family as his subjects. It is to be noted that the drawings of his cousin Camilla evinced a conspicuous tenderness and ethereal loveliness, testimony to his nascent devotion. I had hoped his interest in anatomy denoted he would follow me in practice, but he displayed a profound sensitivity to any creature in pain and recoiled at the first sight of blood. As a parent acutely conscious of his child's singleness, I overly indulged my son's impulses and allowed him to pursue an artistic career instead of apprentice me as a surgeon. My faith in his genius was justified, however, when he was accepted to the Vienna Akademie at age sixteen. The day he departed for the Continent was bittersweet, for I was losing my favorite companion.

"Before leaving Edward made his intentions toward his cousin Camilla known to my brother, and when he finished his studies four years later the banns were published and they married soon after. I was most pleased with the match, for the cousins were truly in love and well-suited for each other. Camilla's twin sister Cassandra served as bridesmaid and attended her faithfully. The twins were quite close, as may be expected, and as children delighted in demonstrating that bond unique to those who shared a womb, wherein one proves knowledge of the innermost thoughts of the other, without a word spoken. To wit: someone such as their mother, or I, or

Edward, would suggest a word to Cassandra, and
Cassandra had only to think of the word and Camilla
would cry it out. They delighted in this game, much to
the consternation of their minister father, who would
rather they not exhibit their psychic connection so
publicly, fearing more the disapproval of the
Presbytery than the Lord who bestowed the gift upon
them.

"I will describe in detail one instance for
purposes that will become clear. My brother and I
were not close growing up, there being a difference of
ten years in our ages as he was the product of our
mother's first marriage and I the second, but became
so after our children were born, our homes but a half-
mile apart. As Frederick's wife Elizabeth experienced
a most difficult confinement and accouchement, the
new parents made the decision not to produce more
children. And so, deprived of siblings, the cousins
grew up more brother and sisters. We went on holiday
together each year, at Bath. One season Cassandra
pleaded with her father to allow her spaniel puppy
Dickens to accompany the family to Bath, and he
consented. The first night at the resort Dickens ran
away and, unknown to her parents, Cassandra
followed him. She was soon lost in the Cotswolds.
When the child did not appear at supper an alarum
was raised and a party of searchers assembled, but as
it was coming on full dark, it was determined the
rescuers should set out at first light.

"Although the weather was mild, the girl was
but twelve years old, and unused to the out-of-doors.
We put the other children to bed and prepared for a
night of prayer. Elizabeth was close to hysteria and
several times would have slipped out to search for her
precious daughter under the stars, especially after the
naughty spaniel returned without his mistress, had we

93

not restrained her. We were debating the administration of laudanum when the missing girl's twin appeared in her nightclothes at the top of the stairs.

"I shall never forget my niece standing in a moonbeam streaming in from the hall window, her limbs trembling, her cheeks flushed, her blue eyes wide with emotion, a nimbus created by the luminescence behind her surrounding her tousled hair.

"'Where are you, sister, where are you?' she said. 'Where are you, sister, where are you?'

"At this we all started, as much at the transmission as at the message, for Camilla spoke in the voice of Cassandra. That it was Cassandra we could not deny, for the girl suffered a slight impediment of speech that endeared her to all. Camilla repeated the communication, and when she was sensible again insisted on transmitting a message in return.

"After attending to her modesty, she composed herself in front of a mirror and stared deeply at her reflection. We were held motionless while she said in a voice not unlike that of their father, 'Cassandra... Cassandra... At first light look for the stand of yew trees... the grove we saw on the way into town... Choose the best tree... Climb to the top... Look for the spires... the spires ...' She repeated the message and again a third time. Any fears we harboured for Camilla's mental state were unfounded, for afterward she was clear-headed and ebullient, and comforted her parents as only a daughter can. My brother dismissed the incident directly, but his wife immediately calmed, and laudanum was not necessary.

"A little after dawn Cassandra appeared on her own, none the worse for the wear, and reported the location of a runaway horse she spotted from her vantage atop a yew tree. She informed us she spent the night on the ground uncovered, but had happy memories to warm her, and kept the image of a reunion prominent in her mind. She even managed to sleep, images of the Abbey dominant in her dreams, and absorbed her sister's instructions. Upon her safe return, after many hugs and kisses, the child accepted an appropriate punishment for the trauma she caused her mother and sat on a pillow for several days.

"There are other instances of such psychic communication, although none so profound as the one I shall describe.

"I was overjoyed when Edward and Camilla set up housekeeping with me after their marriage, and that joy was increased one hundredfold when Edward announced Camilla's gravidity. In addition, by this time Edward's reputation for portraiture had grown beyond our little community, and he was commissioned to paint Lady Buxton. Our elation at these tidings was sobered only by the absence of the girls' mother, who had been called home several months previous.

"As Camilla and Edward prepared to leave for an extended stay in London, for the Buxton sitting was expected to occupy some weeks, Cassandra fell ill. Camilla of course wished to remain in Chipping Gladden and minister to her sister but Cassandra insisted her place was with Edward, and I volunteered to attend her myself.

"It was as if the poor child was infected by an exotic insect. She presented severe chills, high fever, profuse sweating, nausea, headache, et cetera. Dr. Purefoy, the family physician, diagnosed ague or

95

influenza and prescribed total bed rest in a darkened room, as she was photo- and phonophobic as well. The patient also exhibiting dermatitis and intermittent convulsive fits, and there being no incidence of seizure in her medical history, Dr. Purefoy suspected dropsy of the brain and, demonstrating that humility common to country practitioners, hastened to London for consultation with physicians more expert in such matters. While there he advised Edward and Camilla of these sudden events.

"Cassandra appeared to be resting comfortably, although her symptoms persisted. After another occurrence of convulsion and subsequent syncope, the familiar shallow and rapid respiration did not recommence. Nurse wiped the sheen from her forehead. It did not return. A radial pulse was not found. A pin was applied to the plantar surface with no result. Nurse held a mirror to her mouth. No condensation materialized on the glass. The pupils remained fixed and dilated. Still we waited for this sweet daughter to revive.

"The carotid artery was palpated with no detection of the cardiac cycle. Auscultation demonstrated no respiration. A vestibulo-ocular reflex test was unsuccessful. The patient voided her bladder. My brother was apprised his daughter had passed; he accepted the news with stoic compliance to the Lord's will.

"Meanwhile, my son and his wife had returned from London and I shared the terrible news with Edward. He took upon himself the task of advising Camilla that her sister had joined their mother in God's abode, whereupon she gave a dreadful cry and collapsed, and we feared Providence would remove her, also, as much comfort as it would be for the sisters to waken in Eternity together. In some few minutes she revived and asked, 'Is it true? She is gone? Is God so cruel He would rip me in two?' and fainted in Edward's arms. He immediately ushered her to bed lest the shock of such traumatic news induce a spontaneous abortion and we lose another precious child that day.

"Our beloved daughter was laid to rest that very eventide, as the cause of her illness yet eluded us and we feared contagion. It was deemed best that only those exposed to Cassandra during her final days prepare her for burial, and thus Camilla was denied that awful yet strangely comforting task. Nurse bathed the dear child in warm water, then wrapped her in the finest white linen and laid her mother's silver cross upon her breast. Her father conducted a brief service and the simple pine box descended into the ground. But Camilla refused to leave her sister's grave. We at last removed her with soft words and gentle tuggings.

"It is here my story becomes exceedingly stressful to relate.

"That night after the service, as Edward and I prayed for Cassandra's immortal soul and an easement of the suffering of her sister and a father who grieved alone, Camilla appeared at the top of the stairs much as she had that eventful night at Bath some years before, trembling with excitement, her eyes wide and bright, a nimbus again surrounding her hair.

"'It's Cassandra!' she cried. 'She's alive!' and fell against the balustrade. Edward rushed up the stairs and would sweep her into his arms but she pushed him away. 'No!' she protested. 'She will speak!'

"And then, as her fingernails scratched a tattoo on the banister, she spoke in the unmistakable voice of her twin:

97

"'Camilla, Camilla... Hear me... I am alive... I yet breathe... Feel my thoughts... I am on this side... Come and rescue me... Honey dear, Camilla, you heard me when I was lost in the Wilderness and brought me home... Hear me now... Come for me...

"'I have not long... I am weak... I can't... My fingers are bleeding... Camilla... Camilla... What? You have heard me! You have come for me! I hear you digging above me. Dear Camilla! You are here! I am rescued!'

"At this, when any other psychic agent would have collapsed, Camilla bolted down the stairs and flew out the front door. Edward ran after her to the stable and found her harnessing her pony for the trap. They mounted quickly and raced past me as I exited the house. I knew where they were going. The cemetery was not far.

"They would need help. I threw a lantern and shovel in the wagon and hastily bridled Monty, our draught horse. There was no time to wake the servants for more hands. We would do this alone.

"As I approached the cemetery a wagon with two men at the reins hurtled past me, almost upsetting my vehicle. A moment later I encountered Edward's trap overturned where the road sharply curves, the pony struggling to stand. I righted the trap and pony and found Edward crawling twenty yards from the road, dragging his left leg. I stopped him and quickly diagnosed a comminuted fracture of the distal femur. There was no sign of Camilla.

"'She's out there!' he cried. 'She's gone to Cassandra!'

"I started after her but Edward insisted on accompanying me. I could not refuse my son. I lifted him and slung his arm over my shoulder. I made him carry the shovel and managed the lantern myself.

98

Together we hobbled toward Cassandra's grave and an uncertain fate.

"I cannot call to mind our discovery without shuddering, even as ten years have passed since that night. When we arrived at Cassandra's grave, no one was there. Both girls were missing. The hole yawned before us next to a mound of excavated earth; the coffin lay in pieces. I held the lantern and inspected it. It had been hacked open as with the blades of shovels. Bloody claw marks gouged the inside of the lid and a silver crucifix lay embedded in one of the scores. Edward absorbed the meaning of the scene. With a cry he collapsed insensate and remains so to this day.

"For while Cassandra endured that most sequestered of purgatories and attempted to claw her way out, while Edward and I petitioned the Lord to bless and keep her immortal soul, and even as Camilla awakened with her clairvoyant message, those most heinous of criminals crept onto that sacred ground and plied their abominable trade—that of resurrecting the presumed dead.

"It was these ghouls Cassandra heard digging and mistook for her rescuers. With what rejoicing did she greet her liberators, and with what confusion and terror did this innocent child receive the fatal blow?

"We may conclude from the evidence that hardly had these desecrators raised her to the surface than Camilla interrupted them. If Cassandra was still breathing when the fiends broke open her coffin, they soon dispatched her and turned on the one who would stop them. We may be certain neither daughter left that graveyard alive, for these ghouls are not paid for living souls. They train a horse to amble along the country lane drawing a harmless-looking wagon while they pursue their nefarious chore, and it was their horse meeting Edward's speeding trap that startled his pony and he was flung to the ground. The miscreants recovered their wagon after concluding their ghastly business, and it was this vehicle I encountered mere yards from the gravesite. Had I only known the precious cargo it transported! Our sole consolation is that these dear girls spent their last moments together and faced their Maker hand in hand.

"Inquiries disclosed no female cadavers were accepted that night or the next at any public or private college, school, or teaching hospital in this part of England. We extended our search northward and into Scotland to no avail. Reports reached us months later that two young women in remarkable health, one bearing a child, were the subjects of a dual autopsy in Leiden that spring. A Karolinska anatomist divulged he would readily expend a premium for such sisters, for their instructional value in tandem would be incalculable. For my darling nieces to be prized only in death is beyond devastating, and for their dissected remains to be disposed of in a basement furnace without ceremony—to be received in Heaven without benefit of a Christian service—is too horrible to contemplate. My brother could not bear this thought; he trebled the anxiolytic prescribed by Dr. Purefoy and left his fate to God's mercy.

"The Anatomy Act notwithstanding, the wicked trade in purloined corpses continues, for demand far exceeds supply. Mort safes and grave watchers will not impede determined burkers. They have devised speedy methods of exhumation and distraction to avert suspicion, as we have seen.

"Much attention is given to premature interment and reports of persons rescued from such a fate, but an exhaustive study of the medical literature and regular correspondence with contemporary physiologists has revealed no one so resuscitated has survived longer than a few days. That is small comfort to those who discover too late they have buried a loved one prematurely, who are fully cognizant that a lifetime of remorse is scarcely commensurate with the terror of asphyxiation suffered alone in the darkness of the grave.

"I am no longer brother, uncle, or father-in-law, and the role I most looked forward to—that of doting grandfather—I shall never play. These happy functions are denied me. And I am forced to consider this: had Cassie been cremated—even if the flames consumed her as she yet breathed—our family would be spared this heartache and horror. I am as certain as God made Adam that if my niece had known by some Heavenly divination what would transpire upon her premature interment, even if she had awakened as the flames licked her feet, she would choose a living inferno to a living inhumation, to murder and abduction by these ghouls, to her dear sister and her unborn baby suffering the death blow at their hand, to her sweet brother-in-law adrift in a twilight consciousness from which he shall most probably never return, and to her father risking his immortal soul by the taking of his own life.

"The one role left to me is father and I humbly accept it. As I stand before you autonomous and in possession of all my faculties, my beloved son awaits me at home, imprisoned within a corporeal shell, insensitive to all importunities, condemned to an unjustifiable internal purgatory, the extent of which is known only to the Creator Himself. Edward is thirty-one. He is possessed of excellent physical health and is expected to live another thirty years. I am sixty years old and have at best a dozen years to reach him. I am proud of my son. He has endured unspeakable abomination and tragedy, and I vow to see him smile once more before I am called."

At this Mr. Upton bowed and quit the stage, leaving his listeners stunned and horrified. Any expression of sympathy for this man's travails would be plainly deficient; nonetheless, this reporter voiced his deep condolences and admiration which the speaker accepted with gracious sincerity. He was asked whether he still practiced medicine.

His answer: "I shuttered my practice ten years ago."

This reporter assumed the care of his son consumed most of the surgeon's days and nights, but could not help but ask why.

His reply: "Can you not guess? Dr. Purefoy was not available during Cassandra's last fever. I am the one who pronounced her dead. I caused all this horror and torment." And then: "What are the fires of cremation to what I shall endure for eternity?"

Illustration by P. Emerson Williams

The House that Jack Built

by K. Scott Forman

2 November 1898

Dear Nephew,

I tell you this tale in the hope that you will understand why I have isolated myself from your life and from the very commerce of mankind. I have hope that, once you have read my story, you will understand why I am the way I am, and why I do what I must do.

A thing I cannot explain haunts me. It hunts me in the cold dark streets and alleys of London, looks for me in the warm pubs of Whitechapel, and even watches me while I sleep. I write with the hope that no man or woman should suffer what I have suffered these many long years. These jots and tittles may seem the ravings of a madman, a lunatic, but they are true, as sure as I write them, and as sure as I breathe.

It was a decade ago, about this same time in early November. I found myself in the sorry state of rich knowledge and poor funds when I met the man who would become my benefactor, and my curse. Sir Randolph Willard Rasmussen was infamous in circles unreachable to most. He was also the common man's friend. I had known of him, but this dark night we would become intimate.

I crossed paths with this aristocrat and knight, Sir Will as he was known to those of us in lesser circumstances, in an old pub in Whitechapel: the Ten Bells. Sir Will was wont to frequent pubs and taverns of each district in search of companionship and solace. He had a well-known condition – a troubled conscience, melancholy – that would crush even the most ardent in faith. Even those without scruples or moral compass would take pity on the man whilst he suffered from his condition.

I was gathering my writings and wondering where I would spend the night, or who would offer me work, when Will offered a round to the house. In my pauperized situation, I was more than willing to imbibe in a pint, as well as spend another hour with a roof over my head in relative warmth. I thanked the old gentleman, and soon I found myself telling my story of misfortune to a man I had just met.

My life had seemed the same for many months, and Will was empathetic. I was surprised at his understanding of the life of a writer, a constant student, scraping by on barely enough to eat, let alone, drink. The discussion continued into the more obscure literature, verging on alchemy and worlds beyond our own. I had written several pieces on other dimensions that had appeared in the rags around London, and was surprised that Will was familiar with them.

"I knew your grandfather, Martin, and I know your heritage."

His eyes fixed on mine as if we were more than acquaintances, as if some dark and secret knowledge bound us. I knew my heritage, more myth than material. Before I could question him, he changed the subject.

"What do you make of the recent killings?"

The question was valid, but unrelated to our ephemeral topics up to that point. The recent series of murders had left the police puzzled and without suspect.

"Tragic," I said, "and inhuman."

"Yes," said Will.

I was taken for a moment by the passing shadow in Will's eyes, or the pallor that appeared and disappeared on his face in the blink of an eye.

"Almost supernatural, as if—"

Sir Will paused, as if recalling something better left unspoken, and then continued.

"Natural or super-natural, forces indeed, that can take the life of a man or woman drop by drop. Do you feel it? A companion that hides in all humans, but only strikes when the time, the situation, allows, and when the stars are right."

I was struck by wonder, and then fear. My grandfather had said such things.

"Dark writing, myths and legends: I am accustomed to them, know them like history. They are—" Will stopped, his eyes hard on my face. "They are something I know you, my friend, are very familiar with, although you pretend not to believe them."

He expressed a knowledge of some of my tales of the horrific, my cyclopean landscapes; he said they reminded him of Poe. His fascination with the macabre was troubling; his knowledge of things better left unspoken was impressive and disconcerting, but not as bewildering as his familiarity with me.

"Your fiction would be better if your facts were right, but then, who really knows the facts when it comes to the Dance of Death, or if one is trying to unlearn what he has learned?"

It was more a statement than a question. I wanted to ask how he knew who I was, who my family was, but he continued speaking of things terrible and sublime, arcane and distant. Then, the subject returned to the recent murders and the well-published writing of the fiend who had frequented the very district surrounding the pub in which we sat.

The Juwes are the men that will not be blamed for nothing.

"What do you make of that my well-read friend?" Will asked.

I was not prepared to respond. Certainly theories abounded of the murders: graffiti to put the police off the scent, simple anti-Semitism, or even Masonic secret knowledge linked to Hiram Abiff and the three ruffians who ended his life. There was no shortage of explanations, or of suspects.

"I was intrigued by the Masonic link, but I think it is probably just gibberish," I said.

"Isn't the Chief Superintendent a Mason? Arnold, isn't it?"

Sir Will eyed me, fire in his eyes, and then a sparkle, a glimmer of the promise of revelation. I broke the gaze and sipped my stout.

"You have heard the explanation of Juwes, but have you heard the murders have become a conspiracy? Protection extended from the highest levels of government to protect this madman and his family?"

I said nothing. Will continued.

"Those involved are the leaders of this nation, the very elite, the royals, who, by rights, should defend and protect even the most common street whore. Are the lights of Masonry involved, the money of the Jews, or is it all distraction from something grander and much more sinister?"

I had no response, although I was a curious listener to subjects of conspiracy and intrigue. Will's eyes revealed the kind of captive light created by sadness and the heft of the world on one's shoulders, the kind of light on which a few pints had little effect. At that moment I wished to reduce his burden.

"Look around. How many of these people can read, let alone see the subtleties of spelling? This was a message sent to those of us who grasp the deeper meaning of language."

"So," I said, "the Jews, the Masons, all subterfuge for something larger?"

"Larger, yes, and darker; no Jew or Mason has anything to do with it."

Will's tone was certain. He looked around as if someone might hear his voice. The sallowness of his skin changed, and I wondered if he had become unhinged.

"Are you feeling yourself this evening?" I asked.

"I've said too much as it is. I shan't say another word. It's not just me I'm worried about."

"What do you mean?" I asked.

Sir Will would not meet my eyes. Silently, we nursed our mugs to the dregs. I was curious, and I still felt compassion for this man, but my feelings were tempered with the understanding that men say things that mean nothing while under the influence of drink.

"I can feel his eyes upon me, lad. I know when he is near."

"What did you say?" I asked.

"I shall be blamed for nothing."

Will's countenance morphed to mad fear laced with anger. I waved for another round. Will swallowed in large gulps.

"Bring two more," said Will to the barkeep, "and a bottle of my medicine."

He drained the next pint in what seemed to be one large quaff. I sniffed the medicine bottle to find the sweet smells of scotch, but there was something more, something hinting at a backroom brew. Sir Will drank from the bottle; his composure seemed to return, which baffled me. The amount of spirits he

108

had consumed in my presence alone would down a horse.

"Are you feeling better?" I asked.

"Tonight is the night. I can bear it no longer. I have watched you, Martin, for quite some time. Tonight, you have appeared to me, as if by the grace of God. I have a secret, and damn the thing, damn my life, damn it all for revealing it."

I was more than willing to hear my new found friend out, but something on the back of my neck, or deep in my bones, a conscience or a guardian angel, tried to warn me against it.

"Not here, not in this place," he said. "You must come with me; we will go to my study. I can tell you, I can show you. You must believe."

"Are you sure?"

"I'm not turning back. Tonight it ends for me."

He paused for a moment, looking in my eyes. An incredible sadness seemed to creep over his visage and I felt pity. Sir Will pitied me.

"I would not share this burden with any man unless he be willing. Martin, what I have to tell you will change you, could make you become like me. Are you sure you want to hear my tale?"

Again, the prick to flee and never look back, but my curiosity trumped any sense of safety.

"Let us be on our way."

"Good man, Martin."

The witching hour approached when we hailed a cab. We were soon in the warm study of Sir Randolph Willard Rasmussen; politician, philanthropist, and voice of the people. Will was as sober as a man could be, which troubled me. He hurried into a dim room and bade me sit in a comfortable chair facing its twin by the hearth. A fire burnt low. The servants had been dismissed.

Will returned, wiped his brow, looked toward the single window in the richly furnished apartment, and paced, first to the window, then to a bookcase, behind a large desk, and back to the door. I sat silently. Was I watching the fall of a pillar of society into the depths of madness? A clock chimed on a shelf near where I sat.

"Ah, fifteen minutes before midnight. The witching hour draws close. Are you ready, my friend, to hear my tale?"

I acknowledged my willingness. Will secured the lock on the window, drew the curtains, moved to the door, and locked it. He lit a lamp and placed it on a small table between the chairs. He then removed an old black volume from the bookcase, and sat down, placing the book on a small table between us. He opened the book, thumbed through several pages, and stopped, turning the book toward me.

"Do you recognize this drawing?"

I looked at a pentagram, upside down, the downward point aimed at a goat-headed image. I recognized the Eye of Horus at the seven o'clock point position, but the other three symbols at the inverted star's other points were unknown to me.

"Arcane occult symbology; I see the Egyptian, and this fellow must represent Pan, Satan, or whatever you please," I said, pointing at the bottom of the page.

"Yes. The other symbols come from a time and place you can only dream of. The Eye of Horus is our plane of existence, the goat the dark depths of Hell where all points fall. These other three represent other dimensions, other realms, complete with hidden knowledge, secrets, and powers of their own. Would you believe I've been to these places? Seen them? Brought back knowledge that made me what I am?"

I hardly believed a word Will said; although I was sure he believed it himself. I remained silent.

"You do not believe me, and you have long tried to forget the tales of your family. Tonight you will hear my tale and change your mind about a great many things. You will glimpse these places. You will witness my restitution for what I've done, for what I've covered up for so many months, and do what you were born to do. Did you know I had a twin, a brother?"

Will narrated a story of his youth; of a brother he loved dearly, his own ascent up the ladder of success in education and public service, his brother's descent into oblivion.

"My brother strayed from the family path, wasting time and talent studying the obscure arts lost to man, dabbling in sorcery and alchemy, looking for the philosopher's stone."

Where Will was a success in the light of day, his twin was a complete failure. Eventually, his brother disappeared, although he had been purposely forgotten by the family for many years. Will tried to maintain contact; the last word was that his brother had fallen in with a bad lot and died in a den of iniquitous living in a faraway land. Will was devastated. Thus began his melancholy. He was lost without his brother.

"I didn't know what I would do. I spent several years mourning him, but then, last August, without any indication, my brother appeared at my door. He was well-groomed and looked every bit the gentleman in the dark light of night. I tried to embrace him, but he warned me not to touch him. He didn't want to contaminate me with the sickness he bore. I invited him in and he said nothing. I noticed a dark stain on his clothing."

Will's brother told a tale of travel, of discovery, and of losing his soul. He believed himself the servant of a dark power that demanded sacrifice. He had served this power, had been given a key that opened gateways to immense knowledge and sources of power. He did not weigh the cost, and now it was demanding payment. He had little self-control left. He asked Will to release him from his bondage, or else he would cease to exist as John Willard Rasmussen.

"What was I to do?" Will asked. "Who could believe such a story? Having just found my brother, was I to destroy him?"

The question had been asked before. I was remembering my history, tales long forgotten, and my grandfather. There was a king, a sister, an unholy union, and death. I shook my mind clear of the fable.

"What did you do?"

Will had fallen silent. He looked down at the book, then up at the clock. It was a few minutes until midnight.

"My brother had killed a woman."

"What woman?"

"One of the first of the recent killings on August 7, a Martha Tabrum."

I was shocked. I had read about it in the paper, remembered the name, but if this was true–

"My brother told me he was just obeying, but then the power seemed to seize him, consume him, and he feared the next victim would receive a much worse treatment. There would be more killings, payment for what he had gotten himself mixed up in."

"Your brother is this madman?"

Sir Will ignored the question. He looked at the curtained widow and then back at the book.

"My brother had killed before, but only those poor souls who were already near death. It was

112

compassion, a trade off, mercy given to the dying, deaths that would pay the price of his forbidden knowledge, but the evil demanded more, not just human lives, but human lives in their prime. My brother would have to continue killing until his debt was paid. He returned to London for my help, for sympathy at my hand. I didn't understand and asked him to explain."

Sir Will looked at the book that still lay open before me.

"It was the last great secret, the secret to power and riches, the power to enter the forbidden realms, and it was never meant for man."

Its secrets came at a terrible price. Life was the payment for this forbidden knowledge, the life of the recipient, unless the recipient could provide substitutes. The book, the evil it contained, didn't care where payment came from, and the more life that was available, the more willing the book was to assist the debtor, to hide the crime, the sin, as well as open greater secrets, secrets that had similar costs, but it had all been a lie. The evil only needed a pathway into the human world.

There were rules, of course, even evil must obey rules. The killings continued. Will's connections in the constabulary, with the Masons and Jews, kept his likeness and his brother's off the suspect list. His brother's life was ruined. Will's would be next.

"Are you saying you have something to do with the murders?" I asked.

"I did what I had to do. It was my own brother, but now his soul is lost in unknown realms, and his body is nothing but a shell for the evil he unloosed."

Will paused.

"I now know the horrible secret, and so do you."

He looked away, mumbling.

"Johnny, good old Jack..."

Sir Will was remembering the brother that had been, the brother that had left him in the grip of great sadness and remorse.

"My brother is gone and will never return, and I am already chosen as the next victim of this evil curse, the conduit between worlds."

This revelation was more than I could fathom. Will was either insane or the most practical man I had ever met.

The clock began to toll the midnight hour. The temperature chilled. Gooseflesh rose on my arms and legs. I looked about the room as the chimes struck one, two, three...

The lamp went out, the fire dimmed, the air dampened, and the putrid smell of decay filled my nostrils. I felt dizzy, grabbing onto the arms of the chair. The open book before me was the only object I could see clearly. Its pentagram blazed a bright orange, and then smoldered to red, then blue; it seemed to relax its light into a subtle green glow.

"The first time is unnerving."

I heard the voice, but it was distant, the sound bouncing off the sides of a metallic tube finally reaching my ears as hollow and empty. My vision remained clear, but only on the green light; the periphery was black and I had the sense that the darkness of Hell surrounded me.

"Whatever you do, do not let it touch your flesh."

The last words I would ever hear uttered from Will's lips.

The air I breathed sought exit from my lungs, from the room. The symbol turned yellow, then gold, then grew so bright I could not bear to look upon it. I closed my eyes and felt myself slip into darkness. The last chime struck twelve. All was silent, all was black.

A hand touched my shoulder. It was Will, but it wasn't Will. The man before me had Will's face, Will's clothes; he was Will as far as I could tell, but his eyes were not Will's eyes, and they filled like a slow pint with horror and hate. I pulled away.

"Where is Will?"

The thing that stood before me was gaunt, the skin pale and taut against the bones of its skull. Even in the dark light this man was clearly dead.

What had been horror and hate morphed to a blue burning light of evil at the back of the figure's eyes. Then I knew, this thing had been Will's brother, but was now something more, or less. What powers of darkness had wrought this transformation was beyond my comprehension. Here stood the man Will believed to be his brother, his evil twin.

"I see recognition in your eyes," the figure said. "Will is trying to save himself and his brother, but he has only brought me another potential client. Are you planning to deal with me, Martin? I think you have a history of dealing with my kind. I can smell it in your blood."

I was speechless. This thing had caused terror to rain in blood through the streets of London, it wasn't a man, but something infinitely more evil and in the guise of a man, in the guise of Will's brother, John.

I felt the thing's thoughts, it had planned our meeting; its words, poison-laced with calmness and gentleness that unnerved, and who, I could only assume, believed we may become acquaintances, even friends.

"I think you may be different than my other acquisitions, but when you see what I have to offer, you will come to the same conclusion, or should I say, decision?"

The voice was mellow and comforting, but mixed with the sound of broken glass and metal grating against metal.

"No time for that now. We're off to the streets for some jolly fun."

He raised me as if by supernatural power, and before I knew where my legs were taking me, I found myself in a place with which I was unfamiliar. The trauma of the transformation and the late hour of night prevented me from getting my bearing. I was a victim of evil's pleasure.

"If you want to see Will alive, I have until the sun rises to complete my work. By then we must be back."

I was confused. The occult, the transmigration of souls, the rules of this dark game were lost on me. I was falling into a bottomless dream of darkness somewhere between reality and insanity. Whether in my body or out, the remainder of the hours of gloom and depravity became a blur.

I remember a room, a woman; she was beautiful. But then I saw blood, more blood than I could imagine, and the wretched smell of evil and decay imprinted itself on my memory. The stench of the body's contents still overpowers all of my memories, all but one: the voice of John Willard Rasmussen.

"Sit down, my friend, and watch. You will come to enjoy this. Jack will have you back before you know it, and Bob's your uncle."

At some point, I must have fainted. I cannot remember leaving the scene. I awoke to the sound of a crackling fire. I felt as if I had been drinking all night. My skin was damp, a thin sheen of grime coated its surface, and a permanent chill had seeped into my bones. I recognized the room: had I ever left it?

What hideous atrocities transpired, what Providence had blocked from remembrance, I only could deduce from the papers the next day. I did not comprehend the vision. Had I witnessed the most brutal of murders, of rape and torture, or was it all just a nightmare?

Across from me sat Will, just as he had the night before. A pistol was in his hand and the angle of his head on his neck could only mean one thing. What had been Sir Randolph Willard Rasmussen was now the body of a self-destroyer.

I tried to get up, to flee, but I had no energy. I looked around. Only the book from the previous night lay within my grasp. It was closed, but a piece of paper hung from between its pages with my name written on its edge. I reached for it.

My friend, Martin, I see, too late I am afraid, that I have brought you into something I must end. I was weak when the evening began, hesitant. Now I must stop the madness. Take the book. The book is the key. I do not presume the danger has completely passed. I was my brother's connection to this world, and the connection to the evil he brought into it. That connection has been severed, as you see before you. I only hope I may find Jack on the other side of the Great Wall of Sleep.

There is a chance the evil may have connected to you, to your soul. I pray that you did not touch it, or allow it to touch you, and I pray you remember who you are. It consumed my brother, and has used me. I know who you are, or who you were, your family. You are the only one who could take this burden from me. Take every precaution; Do not listen to it, the voices. It will speak to you in dreams, in visions, and when you least expect it. It anticipated I would stop its course, but it has been here before, it is an eternal evil, and it has alternatives.

What knowledge or power my brother may have gained, what secret combinations and blackmail his evil mentor planned to use against me, all are at an end. Forgive me if I have misjudged my actions, and for the position I have left you in.

I would ask you to find some way to destroy this book. I have failed. It will not yield to flame or acid, it will not remain hidden in the earth or at the bottom of the Thames. It was not fashioned on this earth, and I believe it can be destroyed only in the dimension from whence it came. Alas, I was unable to find the solution. Now the burden falls to you.

In a bag next to the table you will find several things to aid you. I have left a map to exit my estate unseen and undetected. You will find my signet ring. I have left instructions for a few trusted associates who are sworn to assist the bearer of my ring financially and will provide you with a large estate away from London. Good luck and God's speed.

Will signed and dated the letter 9 August 1888. A list of three names followed his signature. The killings stopped that night.

Since then, I have dreamed the same dream many times. I feel darkness creeping in occasionally, but I do not believe Will's brother, the vessel that contained the evil, has found his way back. It has been 10 years without incident. I know – don't ask me how – the evil is getting close again and is desperate. I feel its presence when I recall what I saw, and even when I'm not thinking about anything, just as Will said I would. I have written everything here, dear nephew, in case something happens to me, if I disappear, or if the murders begin again, so you alone will know the truth. If I am implicated in any kind of foul play, at least you will know I am guiltless.

I have the book and it has revealed its shallow promises, but much more. It knows my history, our history, and our role in stopping it centuries ago. I believe I've found a way to sever the link between this world and the others and plan to take the book out of this world. I do not know if I will be able to find my way back. If I fail, and the book remains in this realm, the task of keeping it safe will fall to you. I know my sister, your mother, has prepared you for such a task, she has taught you the old ways, the ways of our fathers, of Merlin and Arthur.

I have left instructions with my solicitor. Upon my death, or my disappearance beyond three years, my estate falls to you. I pray that the book is not part of that estate and I find the key to excise this evil from our world. Remember your namesake. In you flows the blood of kings.

Sincerely and with love,
Your Uncle,

Martinus Uther Blacknight

Photo by John D. Stanton

## Who Will Die Tonight?

### by Michael Seese

A cloudy chill begins to find
The diseased confines of my mind.
A creeping madness I cannot fight.
I wonder who will die tonight.

My topcoat buttoned, my gloves in place.
I dare not taunt the mirror's face.
My blade smiles back in the pale moonlight.
I wonder who will die tonight.

I feel at peace in the damp, sick air.
The dark my lover, the streets our lair.
Then she appears beneath sin's red light.
I now know who will die tonight.

I make a beeline. She thinks I will pay.
But my hollow eyes give me away.
She turns on her heel; the bird takes flight.
Does she know she will die tonight?

She quickens her pace, but it's too late.
This time, this place have sealed her fate.
I drive my blade deep and hold her tight.
She falls. Who else will die tonight?

Somewhere nearby a clock strikes one.
The killing spree has just begun.
I slowly swim through the human blight.
So many left to die tonight.

A staggering drunk; an easy score.
An old man, his wife. Tally two more.

121

Four corpses whet my appetite.
How many more should die tonight?

A nurse, a bobby, the next to fall.
(The latter I pin to a ruddy brick wall,
his arm in salute. Eternally polite.)
Perhaps it is time I call it a night.

But on my way home, serendipity croons.
A trio of harlots, feeling safe, immune.
My knife tastes flesh thrice more, with delight.
Sated at last, I kiss her goodnight.

Back in my manse, my twisted black space.
Nine artifacts join my trophy case.
A savage... me? Please! Do not lose sight
Of how many did not die tonight.

Hysteria

by K.Z. Morano

I shouldn't be writing. The doctor said it isn't good for me. But my womb is wandering again. I have been diagnosed with female hysteria, among many other things. Doctor Devitt said it's the cause of my diseased imagination. If that is so, then I cannot wait for my womb to be removed.

My womb dwells inside me, evil in its emptiness. I have long mastered the art of sitting and smiling through gossip and tea, as my wretched womb moves within my body in one of its pernicious perambulations. Of course, I refused to believe it at first, without realizing my stubbornness was one of the many symptoms of my illness. Time and again, I would ask myself: Why can't I be a proper lady?

Oh I've tried. How I've tried! And when Fate handed me a second chance, did I not try my very best to seize it? This second chance came in the form of a letter from a Mr. Weston. According to the letter, I had inherited some property from my uncle. Neither the uncle nor the property I had ever seen. This uncle, from what I'd heard, was very strange indeed. They said he was an unpleasant sort of man who preferred to isolate himself from the world (a trait that's frowned upon in the small country). There were other rumors as well. They said my uncle was quite the antiquarian, with an obsession for collecting arcane objects. Some even said he practiced witchcraft.

Nevertheless, I travelled immediately by coach to Warwickshire where I was met by a carriage that brought me to Whitlock Manor. Upon arriving, I was received by Mr. Weston and a line of servants with liveried coats and powdered hair. Included in the welcome party was a tall, lean man with a contemptuous face. Later, I learned he was the butler and that his name was Hopkins. There was also Mrs. Chatoway, a stern, smartly dressed elderly woman.

By the time I stepped into the reception area, I was scarcely able to contain myself. It was the grandest, most beautiful house in which I had ever been. Upon perambulating the grounds, I decided my favorite part was the gardens with their box-bordered parterres and arbors with vines creeping about them. Mexican dahlias and Cana lilies from the East Indies peered at me from inside their glass prisons.

"The glass protects them from the English rains," Mr. Weston explained.

The statement seemed to prove he was not ignorant of my ignorance. I did not have a privileged upbringing though Mrs. Chatoway (whose purpose, as it turned out, was to educate me) was immensely relieved to find out that I am able to read and write. I didn't, however, know how to draw or play the piano forte. I had no knowledge of foreign languages, with the exception of some gutter French I had picked up from some of my... acquaintances. The tintinnabulation of the supper bell heralded my first lesson of the day: how not to eat. Mrs. Chatoway emphasized the importance of ladies maintaining la petite bouche. So I made my mouth as tiny as possible and gazed longingly upon the parade of roasted meats and pies and jellies.

After supper, Mr. Weston ushered me toward the mansion's vast library where he explained the stipulations surrounding my inheritance. I was to inherit all of Whitlock Manor but I may keep it only under three conditions. First, was that the butler, Hopkins, should remain under my employ. Second, that I was to respect my uncle's wishes for his chambers and the hedge maze to remain locked and undisturbed. Finally, the third condition was that I must never marry.

Of all these conditions, it was the third that made the most sense. After all, if I did marry, Whitlock Manor and everything else that came with it would no longer be mine. It would all belong to my husband. And if we were to separate, I shall be left with nothing, for such is the law. At my age, (I am eight-and-twenty) it is too late to hope for a good match anyway. The second condition vexed me slightly. I thought: If this were to become my home, then why should I be prohibited from exploring it? The first condition, however, was plainly absurd! As much as I disliked Hopkins, I had a feeling that the manservant disliked me more. But then again, who was I to gainsay a dead man's will especially when he'd just left me a very fine fortune. This thought brought to my mind an important subject.

"I beg your pardon." said I. "But I hope I'm not too late for the funeral. I should like to view my uncle's body. Well, since I never met him, though I did have the chance to view a portrait of him in the drawing room."

My statement was greeted by a prodigious silence. Mysterious glances were exchanged between Mr. Weston, Hopkins, and Mrs. Chatoway.

Then, Mr. Weston said at last: "I'm afraid that won't be possible, Miss Highmore. Your uncle, God rest his soul, died during one of his... peregrinations. His body was claimed by the sea."

At that, I had nothing to say. Later, as I lay on the big bed, a vague kind of terror brushed my breast. I felt as though the house hated me.

It wasn't too long before I became aware of the magnitude of the village people's dislike towards my uncle. At church, a few people would greet me at the vestibule but apart from that, no one made an effort at an introduction to me.

"Your uncle was a complex fellow," Mr. Weston explained.

Weary of his circumlocution, I responded: "Yes, I believe my uncle was a difficult old man. But I do not see why I should be as despised."

After recovering from his shock over my reply, Mr. Weston suggested that perhaps I should throw a ball. After all, if there's anything greater than people's love for gossiping about the manor, it's their desire to see what's inside it.

"Very well, then," I declared. "As mistress of Whitlock Manor, I shall satisfy their curiosities."

The first ball at Whitlock Manor was a success. The night was a constant flicker of silk, feathers, gauze, satin, tulle, lace, and tarlatane. I wore a gown of the finest Indian muslin and looked very handsome, though I say so myself. My card was filled that night and I danced with one gentleman after another though Mrs. Chatoway constantly hovered like a hawk. She had warned me beforehand that as a wealthy lady, I would be the target of many adventurers. To this, I responded rather drily that: "It shan't make a difference since I am not allowed to marry."

Everything was going rather splendidly until I went into the cloak-room and overheard one of the young ladies say: "I bet she isn't his niece at all but a woman of ill repute. Have you seen how she acts around the men and her not so subtle coquetries? Most improper indeed!"

126

This was followed by a chorus of gasps and giggles.

"I heard," said another, "that she is actually the old man's illegitimate child."

I felt my womb clench itself into a tight little fist. Hot tears stung my eyes.

"Are you well, Madam?" Hopkins inquired rather disdainfully even as he helped to steady me. I told him I was quite well, just exhausted from dancing and that I would sit down for a while.

But I had lost all interest in the ball and wandered into other parts of the house. In truth, I had merely feigned exhaustion so that I may spirit the key away from Hopkins's person. I clasped it in my hand until the sharp edges cut through my flesh.

I consoled myself with the fact that where before I had nothing, now Whitlock was all mine. Those girls who had been spoiled and waited on all their lives knew nothing. Growing up with just my mother and me, I had to live a life of maneuvers. I'd lied, schemed, stolen, and cheated, and did many other things of which I cannot claim to be proud.

The candle flicked its yellow tongue frantically against the darkness. I examined the cabalistic collection which I had inherited but had been forbidden to view. The collection consisted of rows after rows of relics which, depending on the beholder, could be either infinite vistas of knowledge or one emptiness succeeded by another. It didn't feel right for those objects to be there. They were like the bodies of a thousand dead, dug up from their graves, denied of a dignified resting place and crushed together in a mass tomb, a capharnaum of various centuries and countries.

Along with the rich rugs and delicate porcelains were instruments of carnage and torture contraptions from every era. Portraits and figures depicted creatures of this world and creatures not of this world. On the shelves were skulls of beasts which bared their terrifying dentition and among them were the skulls of humans! I gaped at the grinning grottoes of their faces. I thought to myself that I shan't be surprised if the old man kept a cadaver among his collections. True enough, it didn't take long for me to find a mummified foot, which, according to the label, belonged to the daughter of an ancient Chinese emperor. Gingerly, I fingered the tiny toes that had been broken and folded into a lotus shape to fit the mold of beauty. Even to my inexperienced eyes, it was clear these grotesqueries were worth a fortune.

My attention was soon caught by a massive manuscript bound in black leather. On its cover was a five-pointed star. It lay inside a glass case, indicating it was an object of high value. If it were an ordinary book, the old man would've kept it in the library. I was about to lift the case when I felt something stir in the shadows.

Clank!

It was the sound of metal falling onto the marble floor.

Clank! Clank!

I whirled around and raised the candle to ward off the germinating darkness which threatened to lay its hands upon me.

"Who goes there?" I cried, my heart pounding violently like an animal in the cage of my breast.

I was answered by a final Clank!

It was the last of the locks of an Egyptian sarcophagus which stood against the opposite wall.

The door creaked open, slowly, menacingly... bringing with it a gust of malodorous wind.

I should've run away but instead, as though in a state of trance, I found myself walking toward it. Inside the sarcophagus dwelt a mummified corpse. I don't know what possessed me then but I found myself reaching out to it and peeling, peeling, peeling away the bandages which covered its face. The yellow-brown bindings clung to the corpse like a jealous lover. So I set the candle down and tore away with both hands. I didn't stop. I kept peeling and pulling and scratching even as I felt between my fingers the ichor of the earth's intestines. I had to know... I had to know...

Finally, the face was revealed. Even in its pauperized state, even with the flesh suspended in the act of melting, I knew that face. And I shall know that face anywhere for its features had been inscribed in the insides of my eyelids.

Suddenly, its jaw dropped open and a single word tried to choke its way out of the dead, desiccated throat. Despite myself, I leaned closer to hear. Then, the fragile neck snapped causing it to lean forward so that its face touched mine. The sound forming at the throat seemed to have solidified, taking in a material form—dark and glutinous—pouring out of its mouth and into my face, my neck, my bosom. Worms, writhing... hundreds of them... Cold, clammy bodies crawling their way inside my dress.

I was never the kind of woman prone to screaming and fainting. But at that moment, I did one and then the other.

When I awoke, I found myself in the arms of a handsome young gentleman. I immediately recognized him as Mr. Leander Hillbury of the neighboring Hillbury Hall.

"Ah, there she is," he said, as he lowered me gently onto the burgundy chaise longue.

"Dr. Hillbury here is a medical man," Mr. Weston hastened to explain. Then, not without concern, he inquired: "Good God, what happened in there, Miss Highmore?"

The horror I'd so recently encountered pervaded my memory. I began screaming again, brushing at my face and my chest with frantic fingers.

"Please, Miss Highmore." Mr. Weston soothed. "I assure you, there's no need for such hysterics. The room has been checked and nothing was seen that's out of the ordinary. Well, that is, apart from the strange objects there..."

Hysterics. The word was enough to shake me out of my panic-stricken state. Remembering how my mother had been treated for her hysterics, how those doctors had taken barbaric liberties with her body... The thought of the abasement she had endured was enough to force me to think and speak in perfect calm. Meekly, I allowed the doctor to examine me. He gave me some laudanum to help me sleep but before he left, he obtained my permission to check up on me on the following day.

Apart from hysteria, I also suffer from somnambulism. Perhaps it was the laudanum I took that night, or the anxiety I was experiencing from being in a strange place. As far as I knew, I stopped walking in my sleep when I turned nine years old, nevertheless, when I awoke, I found myself in the hedge maze. The presence of a round, carved Basalt stone hinted it was the center of the maze. It looked like some sort of sacrificial table crawling with runic inscriptions.

The moon clung like a shiny pearl on the satiny bosom of the night. The yews loomed malevolently and all at once, I was struck by the maze's abnormal geometry, as though certain spaces were being swallowed up by massive yet unseen entities. Anxious to leave the maze and the claustrophobic sensation that had begun to take hold of me, I started walking in spite of not knowing the way. I walked faster and faster until I was running. I was certain I wasn't alone.

As I ran, I grew more and more conscious of a shadowy creature that pursued me. I let out a piteous scream though I knew there was no one to hear me. Round and round I ran about the maze, stumbling several times as branches of trees reached out to tear at my nightdress. All the same, whichever turn I took, I ended up at the heart of the maze. This went on until dawn, until I felt the malevolent shadows retreating. It was only then I felt it was safe to stop and break down in tears.

They found me that morning in a state of hysteria. Dr. Hillbury who had, as promised, come early to visit, cradled me in his arms.

"I woke up last night." I began breathlessly. "And I was in the middle of the maze!"

"Shhh..." he said. "It's alright now Catherine. It's fine if I call you Catherine, isn't it?"

After a confused moment, I nodded.

"I beg your pardon, Madam." Hopkins spoke. "But are you quite certain you've located the center of the maze?"

"Good God, man!" said Dr. Hillbury, tightening his arms around me protectively. "This is hardly the time."

The butler apologized hastily.

As hard as I tried, in my awakened state, I was never again able to find the heart of the maze.

Dr. Hillbury and I took pleasure in each other's society. Soon, I grew used to him addressing me as Catherine though he called me Kitty whenever we were alone. Well, almost alone, for Mrs. Chatoway was always there to chaperone me when we went walking or riding. She was always present, too, during my hypnosis sessions. Dr. Hillbury said he'd conducted hypnosis on patients suffering from somnambulism. I found the therapy to be very modern. He was the only one I would trust to perform it.

I didn't know whether it was because of the therapy or because of the doctor but I felt myself becoming better. He was very handsome with his olive skin, luxurious mustache, and thick, almost black hair he kept fashionably short. But it was more than that. He was different from all the other men with their grandiloquent gestures and their violent praises. He was always so plainspoken yet very civil. He possessed plenty of qualities to recommend himself to a woman and yet his looks and even the fact that he had an income of five thousand a year mattered very little to me. Suffice it to say, I had feelings for Dr. Leander Hillbury of which I cannot write.

Of course, I had heard things about him. "As bad as Lord Byron", the ladies had said. I felt, too, that though he was the sort of man with whom any woman may wish to fall in love, he was not a man for love. Nevertheless, whenever he was around, my smiles grew a shade happier. But then I had to remind myself, time and again, that I wasn't allowed to marry.

Furthermore, each time I caught my reflection in the mirror, I'd find myself wondering how a mask could smile.

I tried to pretend that neither the room nor the maze existed. All the same, strange occurrences continued. My feeling that the house hated me was renewed. I shared these feelings with Dr. Hillbury who was always so sympathetic. But there were things I never dared to tell him such as how I woke one morning to find an abominably foul message written on my wall. MURDERER, it said.

The word had been scribed in blood. On the floor was the gutted corpse of a raven, lying face down as though it had died drowning in the soup of its entrails. I couldn't let others see it so I scrubbed the wall clean and disposed of the dead raven myself.

It didn't end there. I kept seeing the word... MURDERER written on foggy mirrors and windows... I would wipe it out furiously with my fists. MURDERER in sooty letters by the fireplace... MURDERER written in tiny pieces of paper tucked inside articles of clothing... MURDERER in secret codes on the pattern of the wallpapers...

It grew so terrible that I began looking about nervously, searching for the word on every window, on every wall, on every piece of furniture. I knew that it was the very same word the mummified corpse had tried to tell me.

I walked in my sleep again. And once again, I found myself in the heart of the maze. But this time, when I awoke, I wasn't alone.

Hopkins was there, still in his linen nightgown and his night cap. He carried with him a gas lamp and a shovel he was using to dig a hole in the ground.

Apparently, he believed treasure was buried there. He'd meant to dig out the treasure and then bury my body in its place.

"The master'd always been so particular 'bout this maze." Hopkins's refined accent had vanished. "Even more so than that curious room. I've served the old man all my life and when he finally pops off, what do I get? You're a bricky girl, you are, but I always could tell if there was skilamalink goin's ons."

I begged of him to allow me to return to the house. I told him I would leave him to his business and give him all the money he wanted.

His laughter rang, false and horrid. "Let you leave, you say? And risk you callin' 'em mutton shunters on me? You better shut yer sauce-box, miss."

He took one menacing step towards me and raised the shovel with every intention of striking me. But before I could even scream, a figure sprang at him.

The shape of its body shifted continuously under the moonlight like clay under running water. Its size was that of a small child's... a malignant child of the night birthed prematurely from the womb of the inner earth. Its features appeared to be melting, somewhere between a state of development and decay. Nevertheless, despite its unsheathed pink flesh, I was able to see the uncanny resemblance to the man in the portrait which hung in the drawing room.

The skinless foetal-like monstrosity sank its sharp teeth into Hopkins' throat, tearing the flesh, issuing forth spouts of bright red blood. Its knife-like talons dug into the man's torso, sundering it. When the vile creature set its small, pupilless eyes upon me, I saw ages beyond ages in their depths. I knew then he was as old as the antiquities that dwelt in his chambers.

I struggled to break free from the paralysis that imprisoned me. I grabbed the gas lamp and hurled it at the abominable fiend. It gave off a frightful shriek of loathing and lament as it dashed blindly into the bushes, precipitating a conflagration which soon spread throughout the maze.

In the hedge maze, nothing ran straight. Everything curved and split and branched and twisted and interlaced. I could've gone on and on and still end up where I began. Thankfully, Hopkins had tied a rope at the entrance of the maze. I ran as fast as I could, using the rope as my guide and never looking back. When I finally reached the gates, a scream of immense relief ripped itself from my throat. The windows of the house lit up like startled eyes and I knew help would soon arrive.

At the inquest, everything I said was taken with a grain of salt. According to the authorities, only one body had been found and that was of Herbert Hopkins. Only Dr. Hillbury seemed to believe me, or if not, at least he didn't look at me as though I had gone completely mad.

"The man was a veritable thief," he told me. "According to the investigation, he'd been secreting some of your uncle's relics and selling them underground."

An idea struck me. The relics! I asked Dr. Hillbury to accompany me as, for the last time, I went inside that evil room. I took the peculiar leather-bound manuscript from its case. Although the authorities had dismissed the fire as a fortunate accident that prevented my murder, I was determined to prove, at least to myself, that the creature in the maze existed. Furthermore, I was determined to prove that the awful creature was none other than the former master of Whitlock Manor. In truth, I was badly in need of an explanation, even if it were as ridiculous as a sorcerer's dark spell gone awry.

"Well, how are we to read this?" Dr. Hillbury said good-humoredly. "The whole book has been written in some foreign and forgotten language."

I suddenly had a feeling he'd been indulging me and never truly believed I saw what I saw. Nevertheless, I didn't need to understand the words in the book. I merely had to look at the illustrations.

With steadily mounting dread, the understanding of the monster's intent bloomed inside my head. On one of the pages was a ghastly depiction of the very same creature I saw that night. On the very same stone altar lay a naked woman with her legs spread wide apart as if to give birth. The woman, however, was not pregnant. Instead, the horrible creature was poised to crawl inside her womb in a kind of reverse childbirth.

I couldn't bring myself to rest not knowing what the writing on that page meant. For my sake, Dr. Hillbury consulted one of his friends, a Cambridge man who was knowledgeable in Old Latin. He interpreted the subscript for us. It translated loosely as Spell for Rebirth and Eternal Life.

I knew I couldn't bear to remain in Whitlock Manor for another night so I hastened to pack my belongings. How much Mr. Weston or Mrs. Chatoway or the others knew about the true nature of my uncle, I didn't know. All I knew was that it wasn't safe for me to be in that place.

"You cannot be serious!" I jumped at the sound of Dr. Hillbury's voice. His figure filled the doorway to my bedchamber. "After all you've been through, you can't just let some bugaboo scare you off."

"It was no imaginary creature." I bristled, suddenly feeling the need to defend myself. "You must believe me…"

"Oh but I do, darling, I do." My heart hammered faster and faster as he ventured to enter my room and took my hands in his. "Which is why you must marry me."

I didn't know what to say. There's nothing in this world I would've wanted more.

"Come now, what do you say, Kitty?" he said amiably. Then just like that, his voice took on a dangerous tone. "Or shall I call you Hetty?"

I gasped.

"That's right." he continued, taking full advantage of my speechlessness. "I know all about you Henrietta Thorpe."

My mind whirled with images and a word… MURDERER…

"It was you!" I cried.

He shrugged. "And Mrs. Chatoway. She was present in the hypnosis sessions too, remember. I had to promise the old woman a slice of the pie."

"So this is about money." I murmured, still taken aback by the suavity with which he shifted roles.

"Of course." Contempt whispered beneath his voice.

"But you have five thousand a year…"

"And debts. Unfortunately, I enjoy playing whist and the demon of gambling is hot upon my bosom."

"I refuse to marry you." I tried my best to look dignified.

He laughed and his features relaxed. For a moment, it was as if he were once again the man I loved. "Shall I call the authorities, then, Hetty?"

In response to my powerless silence, he smiled and kissed my cheek. "Good. Then we shall wed within a fortnight, my sweet."

Though I have been a constant victim of life's vicissitudes, I have never felt as ill-used as I had that moment.

I suppose by now, Leander Hillbury has squandered away most of Whitlock's fortune as men such as him are wont to do. I suppose someday he'll pay dearly for his transgressions. No sin goes unpunished. Which is why I've grown to accept my punishments in this Magdalene asylum where I've been condemned by my own husband. He'd accused me of adultery when it was he who frequently philandered. What was I to do? It was his word against mine. A doctor's word against a madwoman's... a man's word against a woman's.

Time and again I've wondered what would've become of me had I not met Catherine Highmore. Throughout the journey, she'd kept telling me-- a stranger-- about this mysterious uncle and the fortune she had inherited from him. And I thought to myself: Why should this girl be given a second chance and not I? What makes her so different from me? The answer was: Nothing. And so the evil idea formed itself in my head.

Catherine Highmore was a lovely girl. But she was very sickly and I doubted she would make it to the end of the trip. So I gave her a tonic which the girl, completely without guile, took from me gratefully. I had laced the tonic with ample amounts of belladonna, which I always carried in my toilet chest to make my pupils big and bright. It was good for business. Men seemed to like it that way.

The belladonna served its evil purpose. She grew more and more ill as the journey continued. She died when we changed horses in a small town filled with miners and colliers. The smoke was so thick no one even noticed the body of the woman left behind. I then proceeded with my journey to Warwickshire with Catherine Highmore's papers on my person. I shall never forget her face... those features that had been inscribed in the insides of my eyelids...

This is my story. And it's more chilling than any of the penny dreadfuls I've read. This is what it's like to be a woman in this time. I feel like no woman at all. I am neither male nor female. I simply feel as though I do not exist. Even my body never truly belonged to me. Not while I worked in a fancy London brothel as a whore. Not even when I became mistress of my own manor. Someone or something is always trying to take possession of it.

My body is a haunted house. My eyes are windows from which the ghosts of the past and present can be glimpsed. Their collective screams are trapped within me and each day, it becomes increasingly difficult for me to silence them. Oh but they must be quieted... if I am ever to become a proper lady.

I must stop writing now. Doctor Devitt says it is the writing that's making me worse. Tomorrow, I'm scheduled for surgery. He said it's because the prescriptions and the pelvic massages he has performed are not enough to stop my symptoms. The doctors believe that removing the organ will cure me. I do not care what they think. I hardly know whether I'm sane or insane. All I know is that if my sex is the cause of all my sufferings, then I cannot wait for my womb to be removed.

# Bios

## Sheldon Woodbury

Sheldon Woodbury is an award winning writer (screenplays, plays, books, and short stories) living in New York City, where he also teaches screenwriting at New York University. His books include "Cool Million" a how to guide on high concept screenwriting. His screenplay "The Book of Magic" won first prize in the Maniafest horror screenwriting competition. His latest short stories are "Bones in a City Graveyard" in *Bones 2* (James Ward Kirk Publishing), "Dirty Minds" in *Serial Killers Quattuor* (James Ward Kirk Publishing), "The Halloween House" in *One Hellacious Halloween* (Horror Novel Reviews), "Family Affair" in *Clerics, Charlatans & Cultists* (Gothic City Press), "Last Call" in *Shots of Terror* (Angelic Knight Press), "Payback is a Bitch" in *We are Dust and Shadow* (James Ward Kirk Fiction), "Between Heaven and Hell" in *Demonic Possession* (James Ward Kirk Fiction), "Holy War" in *No Sight for the Saved* (James Ward Kirk Fiction), and "A Beautiful Horror" in *Hell II: Citizens* (James Ward Kirk Fiction). His flash fiction stories have appeared many times on the website Hellnotes (JournalStone Publishing) and other stories on Popcorn Fiction (Mulholland Books) and Horror Novel Reviews. His article "Heroes that Rock" appeared in Writer's Digest® Magazine. "The World on Fire," his horror novel, was published September 2014 by James Ward Kirk Fiction. His story, "A White Farewell with a Splash of Red" will be included in *Once Bitten*, a forthcoming anthology from KnightWatch Press.

## DJ Tyrer

DJ Tyrer is the person behind *Atlantean Publishing* and has been widely published in anthologies and magazines in the UK, USA and elsewhere, most recently in *Amok!* (April Moon Books), *In Creeps The Night* (J.A.Mes Press),*State of Horror: Illinois* (Charon Coin Press), *Steampunk Cthulhu* (Chaosium), *Tales of the Dark Arts* (Hazardous Press) and *Cosmic Horror* (Dark Hall Press), as well as in *Sorcery & Sanctity: A Homage to Arthur Machen*(Hieroglyphics Press), *All Hallow's Evil* and *Undead of Winter* (both Mystery & Horror LLC) and *Fossil Lake*(Sabledrake Enterprises), and in addition, has a novella available in paperback and on the Kindle, *The Yellow House* (Dynatox Ministries).

DJ Tyrer's website is at http://djtyrer.blogspot.co.uk/

The Atlantean Publishing website is at http://atlanteanpublishing.blogspot.co.uk/

## K. Scott Forman

K. Scott Forman is an eclectic writer with dark tastes - suspense, horror, fear. In addition to the prose of Poe and Lovecraft, the poets Blake and Coleridge strike a passionate chord in his heart. His work has appeared in Morpheus Tales and the anthology *Old Scratch and Owl Hoots: A Collection of Utah Horror*. He makes his home in the Rocky Mountains.

## Carmen Tudor

Carmen Tudor writes speculative fiction for adults and young adults from Melbourne, Australia. You can find her latest stories in *It's a Grimm Life*, Tales of *Mystery, Suspense & Terror*, and *Fantasy For*

*Good*. For more information, check out carmentudor.net or follow @carmen_tudor.

## **Stephanie Ellis**

Stephanie Ellis currently works as a Learning Support Assistant in a Southampton secondary school but previously worked for many years as a technical author. Her genre fiction short stories have found success in *Massacre Magazine* (Issues 2 and 3) and *Sanitarium* magazine (Issues 15 and 24), as well as in anthologies by a number of publishers including:

Alchemy Press *Kneeling in the Silver Light*
Angelic Knight Press (upcoming) *Demon Rum and Other Evil Spirits,*
Death Throes Publishing *Peripheral Distortions,*
Mystery and Horror LLC *History and Horror, Oh My!*
KnightWatch Press *The Last Diner, Cadaver, Upcoming: Pun Book of Horror, Raus! Untoten!(Vol 4)*
FringeWorks (upcoming): *Dead Man's Tales,*
Visionary Press *Horror in Bloom*
Sky Warrior Books *Vampires Don't Sparkle Volume 2*
PopCorn Horror's *100 Words or Less*

Her poetry has been published in local and national press, Far Off Places Magazine and What the Dickens ezine.

She can be found, together with her twisted nursery rhymes and flash fiction, on http://stephellis.weebly.com/ and on twitter at @el_stevie.

## Brandon Ketchum

Brandon Ketchum is a speculative fiction writer working out of Pittsburgh, PA. He attended the 2013 Cascade Writers Workshop and his work has appeared in a variety of publications.

## Misha Herwin

Misha Herwin is a write of short stories, novels and books for children and young adults. She has always been fascinated by the supernatural and her latest book is "House of Shadows" where time slips and slides and past and present collide. She lives in the UK with her husband and a very demanding cat and in her spare time she bakes muffins.

## David Schutz II

DAVID SCHÜTZ II, a former Shakespearean actor, spent many years on both stage and screen portraying a wide range of characters from Prospero to Richard III, as well as a Rogue's Gallery of villains in the world of independent film and television (playing serial killers, renegade exorcists, Mafiosi, etc.), besides screenwriting and producing independent projects. He retired from that realm in 2012, and began writing Horror fiction. David has been published in several anthologies, such as: "Toys in the Attic: A Collection of Evil Playthings," "Ghosts Revenge," "The Grays," "Cellar Door III: Animals" and "Bones III" from James Ward Kirk Publishing; "Temporary Skeletons"; "Blessings from the Darkness"; "Satan's Holiday" and "Welcome to Your Nightmare"; as well as in "Shadows and Light Magazine," Issues 1 and 2," and the soon to be released "Lovecraft After Dark" from James Ward Kirk Publishing, and "The Darkened Path," from Charon Coin Press. He is currently working on an anthology of solely his own work, "The Interim

People," which will be published by James Ward Kirk Publishing. David is married to Mary Genevieve Fortier, an amazingly talented, successful, widely published award-winning poet. They live happily together in Saint Louis, Missouri.

His work has also been featured on Hellnotes.com's "Horror in a Hundred" series (http://hellnotes.com/horror-in-a-hundred-logan-street-by-david-schutz-ii).

David portrays "The Conductor," and narrates James Ward Kirk Publishing's "Terror Train" podcast, presenting every story and poem in the anthology, "Terror Train."
https://www.youtube.com/channel/UCPh7AIwnT48
Oo2xu6Ba_Gcw

For more information, please visit David's Author page on Facebook:
https://www.facebook.com/DavidSchutzIIAuthor
David's Amazon.com page:
http://www.amazon.com/David-Sch%C3%BCtz-II/e/BooIGWAWAC

### Dona Fox
Dona Fox began writing in 1988 and published stories and poems in Eldritch Tales, Haunts, Thin Ice, Cemetery Dance (Issue #1), Beyond, and New Blood. In 1990 she began working at the State Public Defender's Office, researching and writing the life history of the gentlemen on Death Row, from before the inmates' conception through the events of the murder that caused a jury to give them the death penalty. At the end of Dona's workday, she found she

had her fill of horror. She didn't write dark works again until the fall of 2013.

Recently, her work has appeared in James Ward Kirk Publishing, J Ellington Ashton Press, and Horrified Press anthologies. Dona also has a short story and a poem in JWK's Terror Train anthology; the podcasts on YouTube provide the listener with an old time radio show experience.

## Flo Stanton
Flo Stanton's prose, poetry and artwork have appeared in the horror anthologies *Traps, Tales of a Woman Scorned, A Pint of Bloody Fiction, Indiana Horror Review 2012, Whispers of Wickedness, Static Movement, Yellow Mama, Black Petals,* and others. Her book reviews, literary articles, and true crime pieces have been featured in *The Indianapolis Star, Castle Rock, Literally, True Police, Indiana Crime Review 2013* and *2014,* the *Futures Mystery Anthology Magazine* website, etc. She lives in Indianapolis with her writer/photographer husband John. You can find them stalking abandoned warehouses, factories, graveyards, and other haunted sites seeking macabre inspiration. Find out more about Flo at **www.3amblue.com** or follow her blog at http://flo-stanton.blogspot.com/

## Michael Seese
Michael Seese has published three books, not to mention a lot of short stories, flash fiction, and poetry. He currently is shilling his latest work, a long short story / short novella titled *Rebecca's Fall From....* Other than that, he spends his spare time rasslin' with three young'uns.
Visit www.MichaelSeese.com or follow @MSeeseTweets to laugh with him or at him.

### K. Z. Morano

K.Z. Morano is a beach bum who writes anything from romance and erotica to horror and dark fantasy. Her stories have appeared in various magazines, online venues, and anthologies. She is the author of 100 Nightmares--a collection of 100 horror stories, each written in exactly 100 words, with over 50 illustrations.

She blogs at http://theeclecticeccentricshopaholic.wordpress.com/

Facebook page: https://www.facebook.com/100Nightmares

### John D. Stanton

John D. Stanton is a writer/photographic artist living in Indianapolis, Indiana. For the past ten years, John has provided hundreds of images to the small press, electronic and print editions as well as book covers, earning Top Ten Finisher in the annual Preditor and Editor polls, as well as three mentions in Ellen Datlow's "Best of" collections. Currently, his artwork can be seen in *Not One of Us* issue #54, *Indiana Crime 2014* and *Indiana Horror 2014* anthologies, and numerous other publications. Check out http://amzn.to/1KZ1JwB for some books featuring his work.

### P. Emerson Williams

P. Emerson Williams is an artist, musician, actor and writer who works in a creative continuum that draws upon an interest in the arcane and esoteric. His passion is for embodying the mythic in visual media and melding visual art with narrative form. P.

Emerson Williams has collaborated with writers
James Curcio, Nathan Neuharth and illustrated
Bedlam Stories: The Battle Of Oz And Wonderland
Begins, the first novel in Pearry Teo's series Bedlam
Stories. His art has appeared in print and online
publications across the world since the 1990's. As a
musician he has worked with SLEEP CHAMBER,
Jarboe, Manes, kkoagulaa among many others.

You can learn more about his work
at: http://pemersonwilliams.wordpress.com

## Joshua L. Hood
Joshua L. Hood currently lives in Boise, Idaho. He
recently received a B.A. in Anthropology with an
emphasis in Archaeology and is pursuing a career in
the field locally. He has completed most of an
illustration degree as well, and hopes to someday
finish that up. He quit pursuing illustration when I
realized that having a degree in it isn't as important as
having a good portfolio, and that he could save time
and money if he focused on that instead.
He has recently combined the two areas by illustrating
archaeological publications. He is currently doing
work for the State Historic Society as an
archaeological archivist and illustrator for an
elementary textbook. On the weekends he works for
Idaho Black Bear Rehabilitation (IBBR) feeding and
rehabbing local black bear cubs, and on weekdays as a
night watchman for a local insurance company.
You can check out the IBBR website
at http://www.bearrehab.org/
In the future he hopes to stop working multiple jobs
and be a writer/illustrator for the speculative fiction
genre and work in local academic archaeology,
digging in the dirt and writing publications on all

things ancient and interesting. - See more at:
http://www.vertopublishing.com/halloween-
celebration.html#sthash.lbJrXkZA.dpuf